A
THREE-RING
ROMANCE

A
THREE-RING
ROMANCE

SYDELL I. VOELLER

Thorndike Press • Chivers Press
Waterville, Maine USA Bath, England

This Large Print edition is published by Thorndike Press, USA and by Chivers Press, England.

Published in 2002 in the U.S. by arrangement with Sydell I. Voeller.

Published in 2002 in the U.K. by arrangement with the author.

U.S. Hardcover 0-7862-3629-9 (Candlelight Series Edition)
U.K. Hardcover 0-7540-4789-X (Chivers Large Print)

The text of this Large Print edition is unabridged.
Other aspects of the book may vary from the original edition.

Set in 16 pt. Plantin by Myrna S. Raven.

Printed in the United States on permanent paper.

British Library Cataloguing-in-Publication Data available

Library of Congress Cataloging-in-Publication Data

Voeller, Sydell.
    A three-ring romance / Sydell I. Voeller.
      p. cm.
    ISBN 0-7862-3629-9 (lg. print : hc : alk. paper)
    1. Circus performers — Fiction. 2. Animal health technicians — Fiction. 3. Large type books. I. Title: 3-ring romance. II. Title.
    PS3572.O275 H47 2002
    813′.54—dc21   2001036779

Dedicated with love to my husband, Ardell,
and sons, Carey and Nathan

Special thanks to:

Paul Pugh
Director of the Wenatchee (Washington)
Youth Circus

Mike Schmidt, DVM
Washington Park Zoo, Portland, Oregon

Richard Coon, DVM

Marli Lintner, DVM

Chapter One

"Mr. Figaro, where are you?" Lisa Prentice muttered anxiously under her breath. Her gaze flicked from face to face in the busy airport terminal. No one looked familiar.

She checked her watch. Her plane had arrived right on time — actually, a few minutes late. So why wasn't he here? Indecision swamped her. Should she hurry to the luggage claim area, pick up her bags, and call a cab? Or stay put? She remembered what Ed Figaro had written:

On June fourth, I'll meet you in the United Airlines terminal at the Wicker City, California, airport. Dr. Woodstock is happy you've accepted the job offer and sends his regrets he cannot meet you himself. Please find your flight ticket and travel itinerary enclosed. In the event you don't remember what I look like, I'll be wearing a red windbreaker with the Jessell and Stern Circus insignia.

She peered out the floor-to-ceiling

window through a slanting sheet of rain. The runway glistened in the downpour. Slate against gray. The endless span of wet concrete seemed to meld into the equally gray horizon.

"Nauseating situation, eh?" an older man with a British accent said as he followed her gaze.

"I hope it's nothing more than a brief summer squall," Lisa answered politely. "I understand rain's rare in southern California."

He nodded in agreement. "I'm here to meet my great-niece. Traffic was beastly on the interstate —" He broke off suddenly. "Ah, there she is now!"

"Uncle Ralph!" A pretty young woman wearing a tailored white blouse and a navy blue miniskirt let out a squeal, elbowed her way through the crowd, and enveloped him in a hug.

"Have a good visit," Lisa said wistfully as they hurried away, arm in arm.

Their happy reunion only underscored her impatience. Surely Ed Figaro would appear any minute now, she told herself as she sank into the nearest available seat. Undoubtedly he'd gotten stalled in the "beastly" traffic the man with the British accent had just described.

She felt weary. Bone weary. And her head had begun to pound. Her flight from LaGuardia Airport had seemed to take forever. Electrical storms. Crying babies. And now, no Mr. Figaro.

"Today is the first day of the rest of your life," the familiar refrain echoed inside her head. A new beginning. Ever since she'd been a little girl, she'd dreamed of running away with the circus. And now she had a *real* reason for running. She swallowed hard. The big question was, would it all work out?

The rich aroma of freshly brewed coffee wafted from the cappuccino cart on the opposite side of the wide corridor. Though it was tempting to indulge herself, she quickly dismissed the notion. Her nerves were already stretched to the limit and caffeine might only worsen her headache.

She continued to eye the steady stream of people. Edward Figaro. A picture of the head animal trainer at Jessell and Stern took form in her mind. Despite what he'd said in the letter, she knew she'd have no difficulty recognizing him. Mid-fiftyish. Snowy white hair and a smile nearly as large as the big top itself.

Today's journey had all started when Dr. Joseph Woodstock, the veterinarian who traveled with the circus, had written to her.

He was seeking a competent veterinary assistant, his letter explained. Though the job would pay well, it involved many long, hard hours and sometimes unpleasant circumstances. Would Lisa be interested?

More than a year earlier Lisa had helped save a critically ill Arabian horse named Ebony while the circus was on a five-week layover in Madison Square Garden. After watching a show, Lisa had unexpectedly come across the circus vet in the back lot. He was attempting to medicate the uncooperative mare that was suffering from an abscessed wound.

Lisa had quickly introduced herself, given him her business card, then offered her assistance. Ed Figaro's only son, an aerialist named Michael, had been helping out too. After the crisis was over, he'd lingered a while to show her around. It hadn't taken Lisa long to determine that Michael was an incorrigible flirt.

Now given to impulse — a trait that in the past had been both her salvation and her bane — she'd responded to the vet's offer of employment with an unequivocal yes.

Only later had her misgivings seeped in. When the veterinarian spoke of hard work and long hours, she knew he wasn't mincing words. Granted, at first glimpse, traveling with the circus sounded romantic and glamorous. Yet she realized the work *could* be demanding. There would be times, she was certain, they would be hard-pressed to attend to all the animals that needed their care. What was more, Lisa's quick assessment of the circus vet that day told her he might not always be easy to please. She couldn't help wondering whether she'd be his first assistant or merely one of many others who'd come before her — others who hadn't managed to stay in his good graces.

But where else could she bring in the kind of money the circus veterinarian was willing to pay? Though Doc Largent, the small-town vet on Long Island whom Lisa worked for, was like a father to her, he could never afford to match the wages Jessell and Stern had promised. And goodness only knew, her debts were mounting with each passing month.

"Hi, Lisa!"

She looked up. Michael!

His grin widened as he drew closer. He ruffled her short-cropped, chestnut-colored hair. "Good to see you again, Lisa."

"I . . . I was expecting your father, not you."

"Disappointed?" He sent her a crooked smile.

11

"Oh, no. . . ." Why was he flustering her so? "You just caught me off guard, that's all." Her pulse raced. Too much stress, she thought. The past two weeks had been filled with frenetic preparations — giving notice to her landlord, packing, selling her car, making arrangements to store her furniture and other belongings.

He winked. "Looking good, Lisa."

She bit her lip, uncertain how to respond. She wasn't ready for the likes of him — nor any other man, for that matter.

Yet to her astonishment, she realized she'd been sizing him up too. His hair, the color of winter wheat, was perhaps a little lighter than she remembered. It hung thickly, nearly touching his collar. His muscular forearms were deeply tanned, showing off his corded tendons. The fabric of his black T-shirt strained over taut chest muscles.

She heaved a sigh. "I need to find a place where I can buy more aspirin." Hopefully it wouldn't be long till they arrived at the circus grounds, and she wouldn't have to deal with him anymore.

"Headache?"

"Yes." She offered the first explanation that came to mind. "I never seemed to get them before the snowboarding accident."

12

"Oh, yeah." He nodded. "If I remember right, you'd just finished your physical therapy a few weeks before we met at Madison Square Garden. How're you doing now?"

"I'm fine." She smiled. "In some ways, that seems so long ago. Back then, I'd just started working for Doc Largent about a week." During the short time between graduation from community college and her first day on the job, she'd gambled unwisely and tried to get along without health insurance.

Then came the afternoon she'd crashed on the ski slopes and suffered a fractured femur and internal injuries. Though she'd recovered, the medical bills had been staggering. Too proud to accept financial assistance from her older brother who lived in Wyoming — her only living blood relative — she doggedly determined to pay off debt as quickly as possible.

"I hope you haven't been waiting too long," he said as he hefted her carry-on bag over his shoulder and started walking. "Traffic was outrageous. I guess I underestimated my time." His gait was loose and carefree, with the easy agility of a highly trained athlete.

"I've been here a little while . . . but no

harm. Just figured the nasty weather slowed things up." She hurried to match his stride as they continued down the long corridor, weaving their way through a crush of travelers.

He slowed some, waiting for her to catch up. "Pop sends his apologies he couldn't come for you himself. One of the leopards has a respiratory infection and Pop promised Doc Woodstock he'd give him a hand." He pointed straight ahead. "Let's check out that magazine stand. They probably sell aspirin there. Better yet, sit down and relax while I do it."

"Thanks, Michael, but that won't be necessary. I'll go." Already she was digging through her purse in search of her wallet. "Besides, I promised Doc Largent I'd call just as soon as I got in. Why don't you wait right here? I'll be back in a jiff."

"All right." He gave a forced shrug, sensing she needed some space. If Lisa was anything like his sisters, he knew a guy had to tread cautiously. "Take your time."

As Michael leaned against the wall that separated the corridor from a small arcade, he watched Lisa's retreating form. She was still as attractive as he'd remembered. More appealing than ever.

He exhaled slowly, folding his arms across

14

his chest, allowing the tension to ease. *Keep your cool, Figaro,* he told himself. *It won't work. She's a townie, an outsider. She won't last long. Don't forget the other two vet assistants who got washed up in no time. Without a doubt, Lisa's just as naive — maybe even worse.*

The high-pitched electronic sounds of the video games punctuated his thoughts. Why had he agreed to come? Maybe, instead, he should've stuck to his promise to Claudette and found someone else to meet Lisa. His twin sister had begged him to drive Rita, one of the show girls, to the outskirts of town. Supposedly Rita needed to look up a long-lost relative. A phony reason if he'd ever heard one. *Rita might be sharp,* he thought, *but she's not my style. I wish Claudette would stop trying to play matchmaker.*

Lisa emerged again from the crowd, her cheeks slightly flushed. "I caught Doc just as he was about ready to close up," she reported breathlessly. "Now —" She sighed again. "Now I need to get the rest of my stuff in the luggage pickup area."

He straightened. "Which way?"

"Downstairs, I think. At least that's what I overheard someone say.

"I suppose you've had a busy year with

15

the circus," Lisa said politely in an attempt to keep the conversation light.

"Yep. Our schedule can be grueling sometimes. Two to three performances a day while we're on the road; catching up with maintenance and repairs when we hold over in winter quarters." He darted her a cautious look. "Actually, though, last year I wasn't around much."

"What do you mean?"

"I left for several months. I decided I needed to test the waters on the outside."

"Your parents actually went along with that?"

"Yeah, they were cool. Even though they both grew up in circus families, they told us — my sisters and I — they expected us to make up our own minds. Do what we really wanted. The Figaros have performed in the circus for over three generations, you know. Years ago Mom and Pop came from Europe to America to join a small family circus. A dog and pony show, as we say. But their big break was when they were hired by Jessell and Stern."

"So where did you go? What did you do?"

"The first job was on a fishing vessel off the Gulf of Alaska. The second involved selling home health-care equipment to clinics and rehab facilities." They skirted past a gift shop, a small deli, and a group of flight attendants who were talking and drinking coffee from disposable cups.

"And the jobs didn't work out?" she asked.

"The fishing job was seasonal, of course. Though it offered some of the same adventure and danger that circus life does, I soon discovered it wasn't for me." He smiled wanly. "The sales job . . . well, what can I say? The pay was good. I was bringing in way above my quota. But something just didn't click." He turned, meeting her gaze, his eyes earnest. "Maybe it was because I was beginning to discover the grass isn't always greener on the other side of the fence. I was happiest with what I already had."

"You're lucky, Michael," Lisa said after a moment's contemplation. "Some people never do realize that."

Charles, for instance. Her thoughts darkened. Two years ago, her fiancé, Charles Bergman, a corporate lawyer in Manhattan, had suddenly proclaimed he'd found someone else. Someone more stunning. Someone more successful. Someone more than a mere veterinary assistant.

How had she managed to delude herself into believing his reputation as a womanizer would end? Her pain — and their hasty

17

breakup — had been almost unbearable. After that, she vowed the price of a permanent commitment was simply too high.

They rounded a corner, then stepped onto the escalator that led to the luggage claim area. Michael stood close behind. Too close. Her physical awareness of him disturbed her.

"And what about you?" she heard Michael ask. "What have you been up to this past year?"

She shrugged. "Working nine to five. Getting engaged. Getting *unengaged*."

"Unengaged?"

"Yes." She balled her hands into fists, knowing she'd made a mistake mentioning it. She wasn't ready to talk about Charles, especially with someone like Michael. Yet it amazed her how quickly he'd already shared some personal details of his own life.

She managed a smile. "But enough about that. Tell me about your troupe, Michael. I'd like to know everything."

"Well, all right." He hesitated, slanting her a look. "We're called the Flying Figaros. First there's Claudette, my twin sister. Then there's Estelle, two years younger. She's kind of petite and spunky, a lot like you," he added. He broke into a grin and winked again. "Uncle Rudy, my father's brother, works as our catcher. He took over about five years ago after Pop fell from a tightrope, suffered a ruptured disk in his lower back, and was forced to turn to animal training instead."

"So who replaced you while you were gone?" she asked, watching the floor below draw closer.

"My second cousin Bo, who normally travels with another circus. All the time, though, Claudette kept insisting that Bo wasn't working out — which I hate to admit, was probably true." They stepped off the escalator.

"Why?" Lisa asked. "Hadn't he been flying as long as you?"

"No. Not quite. But as far as Claudette was concerned, that was only part of the problem. She never wanted me to leave in the first place. Claudette was afraid the troupe's reputation would fall apart and all our years of hard work and practice would have been for nothing."

"I guess you couldn't blame her for that," Lisa said.

"Right. But you don't know my twin sister. She can get a little unreasonable at times. No matter what I do or say, she can't seem to shake the notion I might decide to split again. This time, permanently."

19

"I've always heard that circus families are close," Lisa said, casting him a sidelong glance.

"Yes. Claudette, Estelle, and I started flying when we were little kids. Even though we have our ups and downs like all brothers and sisters do, we can't help but be tight."

Lisa envied him. She and her brother, the only two children of alcoholic parents who'd spent the best part of their lives in and out of treatment centers, had been raised in a succession of foster homes. All those years she'd always realized how tenuous and fragile her home life could be. Her foster parents might decide the arrangement wasn't working out and send her away. And even if they didn't, she would still have to move on eventually. Lisa longed for the security of a stable and loving family.

Like Michael's.

"Now for your bags," Michael said, leading the way toward the conveyor belt. "One or two? What do they look like?"

"Two. Two big ones." She rattled off a description as she clutched her claim ticket. But as one unfamiliar piece of luggage after the next paraded by, a strange feeling rose in the pit of her stomach. Her suitcases weren't there.

"I'm sorry, miss," the skycap said after

she'd tipped him to investigate further. "Apparently your luggage was rerouted on another flight."

"Great!" She gulped as visions of her bags landing in some exotic foreign airport flashed by her.

"I checked at the desk for details," the man said. "There's another plane due in from LaGuardia in an hour, flight 801. If you'd like to wait, there's a good chance your bags will turn up then."

Lisa sent Michael a questioning look.

"Don't worry," he was quick to say. "I've got plenty of time."

"Are you sure? Don't you have a show to hurry back for?"

"Not today. There's no matinee."

They passed the next hour at the airport deli, sipping sodas and munching on bagels and cream cheese. But after the next flight arrived without her bags, she had no choice but to fill out a missing luggage form.

"I'll put down my brother's address in Jackson Hole and call him first chance I get," she said to Michael. She heaved a sigh of frustration. What was she going to do? Buying new clothes would put a sizable crimp in her budget, but she'd never admit that to Michael. She'd learned at an early age to be as self-reliant as possible.

"You brought a few things in your carryon?" Michael asked.

"Yes, thank goodness. Enough for maybe a couple of days."

"If push comes to shove," Michael said, "and your luggage never does show, maybe Estelle or Claudette can loan you some of their clothes." He turned for a brief moment, his eyes roving over her approvingly. "I think you and Estelle are about the same size."

"Thanks, but that won't be necessary," she said, lifting her chin. "I'll figure something out."

At last they were speeding away from the airport in Michael's kelly green Ford pickup. The subtle masculine scent of his after-shave tugged at her composure. *No, Lisa. Get a hold of yourself. You joined the circus to try to forget what's happened. You don't need another man to mess up your life.*

"Estelle says to tell you that you're welcome to live with her in her trailer," Michael said. "She's got plenty of room and would love the company. The two of you should get along fine."

"I'd like that. At least for a while." She flashed him a smile.

Through the speakers in his CD player, the silky strains of a saxophone played. The windshield wipers moved back and forth with a steady drone. The streets glistened with moisture. Off the freeway, she caught an occasional glimpse of palm trees sandwiched in between sections of shopping malls and business parks.

"Your father said in his letter that my lodging would be provided," Lisa continued, "but I do intend to buy my own RV — maybe a small used trailer — just as soon as I can pay off some bills." She bit her lip. "That is, *if* I manage to stay."

"You mean if you don't pass your probation?"

"Uh-huh. Dr. Woodstock told you what he'd written in my contract?"

"Sure. Doc put the same requirements on the other two assistants."

"Oh." She gulped again. "So I'm *not* the first. I wondered about that."

"There were two. In less than a year." He waved a hand through the air. "Here today. Gone tomorrow."

She wound a strand of hair around her finger as her uneasiness about the veterinarian skyrocketed. "Last year when I was helping Dr. Woodstock, well . . . how can I put it without sounding rude? I got the impression he isn't exactly Mr. Rogers."

"You're right." Michael chuckled. "But in

all fairness, let me say this. Doc's a top-notch professional. He's terrific with the animals, especially the larger critters. If you *can* get along with him and pass your probation, you'll have it made."

"Have you worked with him a lot?"

"Some. When Pop or one of the keepers is busy, I try to help out. So does Mom, though most of the time she's busy training her poodles."

"Well, I'm not worried about anything at all," she said with false bravado. "I enjoyed my job at the veterinary clinic back on Long Island, and I'm going to enjoy this one too."

"I hope so . . . but don't overlook the obvious, Lisa." The doubt in his voice came through loud and clear. "Lions and tigers aren't your everyday house cat, you know." He swung into the next exit, merged with the traffic, and came to a stop at a traffic light.

"Maybe you're right about that," Lisa conceded. "But I'm sure my perseverance and love for animals will see me through. I've been an animal lover since as far back as I can remember. Only problem was, because I changed foster homes so often, I rarely got to have any pets I could call my own."

"Must've been kind of tough."

"Yeah, it was. Though most of the time, I

lived with loving families, I always knew my situation was temporary." She offered him a tentative smile. "I can remember standing in front of pet store windows, wishing and praying I could take home a puppy or kitten or even one of those furry little guinea pigs with the shiny black eyes. Just to have something to love that was *all* mine."

Her words were unraveling him. He tried not to let his feelings show, but it was a tough call. "Didn't you ever talk to your foster parents about that?"

"No. Never. I just figured it wasn't worth it. I was lucky enough they'd agreed to give me a home, let alone a pet too."

As the light turned to green and they were off again, she detected a play of emotions on his face. Sadness. Concern. Tenderness, perhaps?

He reached out and touched her hand. "Cheer up, Lisa. You've finally hit the big time. Now you've got a whole menagerie of pets to call your own."

She couldn't help smiling. "You're certainly right about that," she answered him. "I'll have more animals than all the pet stores combined."

"And time to spend with Ebony too," Michael reminded her.

"Oh, yes! I've thought about her so

often!" The black Arabian was Edward Figaro's most prized show animal. "How's she doing?" Lisa asked. "Did she recover from the infection?"

"Ebony's great." His brows knit together in a frown. "Hopefully she'll never get sick like that again. She had us all plenty worried, especially my father."

"I remember. Your dad was nearly beside himself."

"That's putting it mildly. Pop's got a lot invested in that horse — in more ways than one."

"What do you mean?"

Michael swung into a narrow alley and slowed the truck to a crawl. "Last week my father found out he's been inducted into the Circus Hall of Fame. All because of the tricks he's taught Ebony."

"That's wonderful!" She turned to face him squarely. "When can I see Ebony again?"

"Maybe later tonight after the show."

Michael parked behind a long string of trucks and trailers. But before he came around to open her door, he reached out again to touch her hand. "Lisa?"

"Yes, Michael?"

"After this, I may not be seeing much of you . . . I mean, we're both going to be busy."

26

Her heart turned over. Michael's dark eyes, those deep pools of midnight blue, were driving her insane — and if he kept touching her like this, she might fall apart completely.

"I realize that," she said and swallowed hard. "Just because you gave me the grand tour last year in Madison Square Garden, doesn't mean I expect you to do that this time too."

He hesitated, running his tongue over his lower lip. "Good. So now that we understand each other, there's one more thing. . . ."

"What?"

"Just in case I don't get the chance to say it later, I . . . I want you to know I'm really glad you're here. It's great to see you again." His expression remained closed.

"Thanks." The words caught in her throat. "It's great to see you too."

She averted her gaze, struggling against panic. Maybe she should ask him to drive her back to the airport. Maybe she should say she changed her mind. But no . . . this was the opportunity of a lifetime. She was here now, and that's where she would stay.

She had no choice but to face the consequences.

Chapter Two

The coliseum and surrounding lot covered six city blocks. Everywhere Lisa and Michael walked people rushed about getting ready for the next performance.

As they wandered behind the dome-shaped building, a shiver of excitement surged over Lisa: the pungent smells of sawdust and animals, the deep-throated roaring of a lion, the shrill trumpeting of an elephant. She adored the kaleidoscope of exotic sights, sounds, and smells that only a circus could offer.

In the back lot, they passed by the menagerie tent, animal cages, and trailers. Joey, a cage boy, was tossing the tigers raw chicken while a couple of animal keepers were refilling the watering trough with long hoses. A white-whiskered tiger bared its teeth and stared back at them through the cage. Though the huge cats were captivating, Lisa had to admit it made her nervous just to think about getting close to them, much less attending to their medical needs.

Joey said to Michael, "Looking for your

dad? He's over there, hosing down the elephants."

"Thanks, Joey." Michael flashed him an appreciative smile.

As they drew nearer, Lisa spotted Ed Figaro filling a bucket of water while three leathery elephants crowded in. A young woman was tossing carrots into a baby elephant's mouth, laughing at its antics.

"Hi! We're finally here," Michael greeted them.

Mr. Figaro reached out to shake Lisa's hand, his dark eyes sparkling. "Welcome, Miss Prentice."

"It's good to be here. Please call me Lisa," she answered.

Michael turned to the young woman and proceeded with introductions, though Lisa had already guessed she was Estelle.

"Michael's told you about my trailer?" Estelle asked eagerly. "He's let you know you're welcome to stay with me?" She dropped the bag of carrots and extended her hand.

"Oh, yes! Thank you!" Lisa exclaimed. "But . . . but, are you sure there's enough room? Doesn't Claudette share the trailer too?"

"Heavens no! Not *my* sister," Estelle answered, wrinkling her nose, then giving a

29

quick laugh. "She was the first to move out of our folks' motor home a few years ago." She laughed again, then added, "Though we all thought that was cool — and were a little green with envy — I still have to admit, Claudette can be weird at times."

"Now, Estelle," Ed Figaro put in gently.

"Oh, Papa! I've heard you say it too . . . in so many words, at least."

"Well, I'm sure Lisa's tired from her travels and doesn't need to hear any of this," the older man said. "And by the way, it's almost time for you kids to get to work. Why don't you take Lisa's bag for her and put it in your trailer? Then you'd better get ready for tonight's show."

"All right, Papa." She turned to Lisa and smiled. "And later we've simply got to visit. That is, if you're not too exhausted by then."

"I'll catch up with you in a few minutes, Sis," Michael said. He gave her a playful punch in the shoulder.

"Did you have a good flight?" Ed Figaro asked after Estelle had disappeared out of sight.

"Oh yes, but it seemed to take forever to get here."

"And now you'll have a bit of jet lag too, I'm sure." Focusing his attention back to the elephants, the animal trainer adjusted the hose nozzle. A sudden swoosh of water exploded. "All right, Kiki ol' buddy, hoist up those feet. It's time for your shower."

As the huge animal rolled its eyes and raised his front feet, Lisa burst into laughter. Still, she couldn't help thinking about how soon she'd have to start helping Dr. Woodstock with these massive creatures. Tomorrow would be her first day on the job.

"Congratulations on getting inducted into the Circus Hall of Fame," Lisa told Ed. "You and Ebony deserve it."

His white moustache twitched before he finally broke into a full grin. "Thank you, my dear. But I give most of the credit to Ebony. She's the best liberty horse I've ever owned."

Lisa nodded. Last year Michael had explained that liberty horses were trained to perform "at liberty" — without reins and sometimes without riders.

Michael's father reached for a scrub brush, speaking to them over his shoulder. "My son is giving you a proper welcome, I trust?"

"Certainly." She felt the warmth rise to her cheeks.

"I'm sure Lisa is eager to touch base with Dr. Woodstock," Michael interrupted quickly, before his father succeeded in embarrassing both of them.

Give Lisa a proper welcome? From the very first moment he saw her again, he'd wanted to crush her mouth with his, press her close to him, feel her sweet softness against him. But he couldn't keep kidding himself — he was playing with fire. Though Lisa claimed she understood what Doc Woodstock expected of her, there would be other problems too. The trainers would also regard her with a jaundiced eye. Unlike Pop, who seemed to have taken to Lisa, they'd call her "the first of May," inexperienced and naive. She'd crack under the pressure, then most likely up and leave — and he couldn't follow her. No, he'd already decided. He'd never leave the circus again.

"Doc Woodstock had to drive into the next town to pick up some supplies for the leopards," Ed said. "I expect him back any minute now, though I'm afraid he won't have much time to visit." He gave the hose a quick snap.

"That's all right," Lisa said, perhaps a little too quickly. Meeting the veterinarian first thing tomorrow would be soon enough.

On the way to Michael's dressing room, they slipped inside the back entrance to the coliseum. Several men were hard at work.

Some were checking equipment on the ground while the others were climbing to the top of the rope ladders. The two closest to the door were speaking to each other in a foreign language. German, Lisa quickly surmised.

"Who are they?" she asked Michael.

"They're called riggers — some of the most important guys in the circus. They check and recheck the high wires and trapeze to make sure everything's safe."

"Hey, Michael!"

Out of the corner of her eye, Lisa caught sight of a strikingly tall blond striding purposefully toward them. With her honey-blond hair drawn back in a long French braid and her sleek black leotard and tights, the woman was the epitome of elegance.

"Claudette?" Lisa asked Michael under her breath.

"Yep. I'll introduce you in just a sec."

"What are you doing, still dressed in your street clothes?" Claudette called to her brother.

"Hold on, Claudette. There's still over an hour."

She looked steadily at Michael, never once glancing in Lisa's direction. "So I see the little veterinarian assistant has finally arrived," she said.

"Yes, she has." Michael's voice was strained, but controlled. "Sis, meet Lisa Prentice."

Claudette folded her arms across her chest, forcing herself to meet Lisa's gaze. "Hello."

"Hello, Claudette." Lisa extended her hand, but Claudette didn't take it.

"Lisa's got a slight problem," Michael went on, ignoring what had just happened. "I think maybe you can help her out."

"Oh?"

Michael went on to explain about Lisa's lost luggage. "Maybe you have a few things on hand you wouldn't mind lending Lisa," he said.

"And exactly what is it she needs?"

He was beginning to look a little exasperated. "Ah, come on, Claudette. How should I know what you women need to get through a normal day? Jeans, a blouse or two, maybe —"

"Okay, okay. I get it." Claudette cut him off with a wave of her hand. "I'll see what I can do . . . though she might have to hem up a few things." She shifted her gaze to Lisa and added, "Of course, we can't let Lisa get off to a bad start, now can we?"

"Thank you, Claudette," Lisa said tightly. "But I already told Michael that I'll be fine. I plan to find the nearest shopping mall as soon as there's time."

"Suit yourself." Claudette shot Lisa a condescending look, then tugged at Michael's shirtsleeve. "Let's go, Michael. Time to tear yourself away. Need I remind you, there are more important things to do?"

Michael turned to Lisa and caught her hand. "You gonna stick around and watch the show?"

Beneath Claudette's steady gaze, she looked him straight in the eye and managed a smile. "Of course, Michael. I wouldn't miss it for the world."

Inside the coliseum, Lisa found an unreserved seat and sat down. The band was playing a lively tune. Vendors selling popcorn and cotton candy worked the side aisles.

As the lights dimmed and the music swelled, a rainbow of colors filled the arena. Lisa's meeting with Claudette soon forgotten, new anticipation flowed through her. It was time for the spectacle to begin.

With rapt attentiveness, she clasped her hands together. Animals in bright headdresses and performers wearing sequin-spangled costumes paraded by. Then came the first act, which soon gave way to the next. Lisa laughed with the crowds at the chimps bouncing on pogo sticks, clapped for the tiger jumping through a ring of fire, and gazed in awe at the red-sequined show-girls performing an aerial ballet.

Next the Flying Figaros emerged. Dressed in glittering silver capes, holding hands and smiling their most dazzling smiles, they sprinted into the center ring. In seconds the troupe was ascending the high rope ladder, Estelle sitting on Michael's shoulders. While Claudette began to swing from a trapeze, Michael and Rudolph, perched on high rungs, balanced poles from their foreheads.

In an instant, the blue spotlight shifted back to the two young women. Lisa watched first one, then the other, spin through the air, skillfully performing their famous double somersaults. The most difficult trick — Michael's triple — was only seconds away.

"And now, ladies and gentlemen, children of all ages," the ringmaster boomed, "world-renowned Michael Figaro will perform one of the most daring acts in circus history! The triple somersault!"

A hush blanketed the coliseum. The drums rolled. From somewhere overhead, the spotlights dimmed, casting a dramatic hue over the performers. Lisa's heart pounded. Every nerve in her body stood on end. *Oh, Michael, please be careful,* she silently pleaded.

Michael dusted his hands with resin. Then he began to swing. The intensity was etched clearly on his face. His taut muscles revealed the strength in his torso and upper arms. Last year when she'd witnessed Michael's performance, she'd secretly vowed he was the most gorgeous man alive. Tonight was no exception.

Higher and higher he arched. With a quick thrust, he tucked himself into a ball and whirled through the air.

The drums stopped rolling. Lisa felt her hands grow clammy as she braced herself on the edge of her seat. Suddenly Michael's body straightened and his hands connected with the catcher's. The applause exploded.

"Ladies and gentlemen," the ringmaster hollered, "you have just witnessed the most important feat on the face of the earth!"

While the crowds went wild, Lisa went limp with relief. *Oh, Michael, no wonder you came back,* her heart cried out. His performance was commanding. Michael Figaro was destined for stardom. How easy it would be to fall in love with him — only to end up heartbroken once again. There must be at least a hundred women, watching him this very moment, who would give their souls just to touch his hand. She could no more hold onto Michael than she had Charles.

One by one, the flyers dropped into the safety net, then onto the floor. The crowd rose from their seats and cheered louder as the troupe took sweeping bows, then disappeared behind a royal blue curtain.

Suddenly the beating of hooves sounded. The air stirred as three gorgeous black horses without riders or reins streaked past. The ring seemed charged with their electrifying energy.

Lisa blinked twice. Ebony! The leading horse *had* to be Ebony! In the center of the ring stood Ed Figaro dressed in white and grasping a long whip.

The blue spotlights shifted to red. While the other horses took their places opposite each other near the edge of the ring, Ebony cantered gracefully to the center. She reared up. Like a magnificent mystical creature, she pawed the air. The other show horses immediately followed Ebony's cue.

Step-by-step she led them through one trick after another. Then the lights dimmed as the horses made their exit.

After the show had ended, Lisa hurried

down the broad hallway that led to the performers' dressing rooms. She found Michael outside, laughing and talking with one of the showgirls who'd performed in the aerial ballet. Inclining his head to one side, he grinned charmingly again at something she had just said, then said something back to her that launched her into peals of laughter.

Meanwhile, a huddle of young women dressed in tight miniskirts had congregated patiently nearby. They were whispering to one another behind cupped hands and casting surreptitious glances in Michael's direction.

Groupies, Lisa thought. She darted another glance at the showgirl. And obviously there were plenty of young women *inside* the circus who found Michael attractive.

Suddenly he turned in her direction and their eyes locked. "You were wonderful!" she exclaimed. "The best!"

"Thanks!" He moved quickly toward her and grinned openly.

Lisa flushed with pleasure. Yet all the while she couldn't blot out the disturbing realization that the showgirl was still close by, never taking her eyes off Michael. Exactly who was she?

"Give me a few minutes to hit the showers and change," Michael said. "We'll go see

Ebony, just like I —"

Footsteps thudded from behind, slicing through his next words. Lisa turned around to see Ed Figaro. His face was drawn, his breathing rapid.

"Son, I need to talk to you."

"What is it, Pop?"

Michael's father drew in a ragged breath. "It's about your Uncle Peter in Australia. I'm afraid there's bad news, son."

Ed opened the dressing-room door and motioned them inside. "Please. Make yourselves comfortable. Mother and Estelle will be along shortly."

"What is it, Pop?" Michael's voice was filled with alarm. "What happened?"

"I doubt you remember my brother Peter," Ed continued, looking at Michael. "He was considered the black sheep of the family and visited only once a long time ago. Well . . . the bad news is he passed away quite unexpectedly last night."

"Gosh, Pop," Michael stammered. "That's . . . that's too bad."

The older man's eyes misted over. "Yes. It's especially too bad that you kids never got to know Peter. Now all three of you are grown, without any recollection of him. Anyway, the funeral's on Friday. I'm flying to his hometown in Australia first thing in the morning." He lowered his gaze. "Of course, since he never married or had a family, I suspect there won't be too many folks there."

"And what about Rudolph?" Michael asked. "He's Peter's brother too. Is he going to fly to Australia with you?"

"No, we've already discussed that. We agreed there's no one else who can fill in as your catcher, so it's important he stay." Michael's father paused and blew his nose loudly into a white handkerchief. "Besides, Peter named me executor of his will, so I have no choice but to go. He was a very rich man with a lot of money tied up in property and investments. It may take quite a while — perhaps most of the summer — until I can straighten out the details of the estate."

Michael's jaw dropped. "You mean you'll be gone for all that time?"

"Possibly." He hesitated before continuing. "I have two concerns, Michael, and I'm going to ask your help."

"Uh . . . sure, Pop. Fire away."

"Keep an eye on Claudette, will you, boy? I'm not sure what's happening, but she's not performing up to snuff. I'm suspecting you've noticed too. . . . She seems to be holding back, hesitant."

41

"Yeah, I'm afraid you're right. In fact, she made me kind of nervous tonight. But don't worry, Pop. I'm sure it's nothing. We all have our bad nights once in a while."

Ed sighed heavily. "I suppose so, but I *do* worry. I'm sure you know by now, Michael, I expect the very best from my kids. So promise me you'll practice hard."

"We'll be fine, Pop. I promise."

"Good. Now on to my next request." He faced Michael squarely. "I'm turning over the responsibility of the show horses to you. Since you've helped me in the past with them more than anyone else, you're my most logical choice."

"No problem." A muscle worked in Michael's neck.

Ed's features were etched with worry. "Thanks, son. I know I can always count on you. Now don't let those horses get lazy. And whatever you do, don't let anything happen to Ebony."

Chapter Three

"You still want to see Ebony tonight?" Michael asked as they strolled down a wide sidewalk that fronted the circus grounds.

"Oh, yes!" Lisa smiled up at him. The pale glow from a streetlight illuminated his profile. Overhead, a spattering of stars winked in the cobalt blue sky. A balmy summer breeze lifted her hair.

Until just a few moments ago, Michael had been uncustomarily quiet. Lisa suspected he was pondering his father's leaving and the added responsibilities that entailed. Or was it something more?

They crossed the north side of the lot, then threaded their way among the animal cages, trucks, and horse trailers. In minutes they came to the horse tent and ducked inside.

The sweet smell of fresh hay filled Lisa's nostrils. A horse nickered. She followed Michael past three black stallions and a Shetland pony that were switching their tails as they munched hay.

"Oh, Michael! There she is!" Lisa cried as

she pointed to the end of the row.

"Yep! Isn't she a beaut?" he asked, beaming. As Lisa hurried up to the horse and began stroking her mane, Ebony lifted her head and stared back through half-lidded eyes.

"Ebony! You're beautiful! Just as I'd remembered." The horse's ears twitched. Lisa reached down, picked up a fistful of hay, and offered it on her opened palm. Ebony's snout was velvety soft.

"Instant bonding," Michael said. He grinned approvingly, rocking back on his heels.

"Oh, I hope so. In fact, I'm looking forward to working with all the horses."

"Good, I might need some help.".

"How are you feeling about that?" Lisa asked as she stooped down to pick up more hay. "About taking the responsibility for the show horses?" She straightened again, then turned to look up at him. She watched his grin suddenly fade.

He glanced away. "Scared. Very scared."

"I doubt that your father would've asked you to do it if he didn't think you were capable."

"It's expected of me, Lisa. That's what being in the circus is all about. Most of us, sooner or later, have to wear more than one

44

hat. Pop would still be flying too if it hadn't been for his accident. And Uncle Rudy . . . he not only works as our catcher, but oversees the sideshow most of the time too."

"And here I am, feeling overwhelmed! All I have to do is assist Dr. Woodstock and pass my probation." A ripple of excitement overshadowed Lisa's uncertainty. Tomorrow. Tomorrow she'd finally set out to accomplish what she'd come for.

"Back home, my best friend Melanie and I go riding almost every weekend at Doc Largent's stables," she went on. "Will you let me ride Ebony sometime soon?"

"Maybe tomorrow. If you can find a minute or two to spring free, just check with me or one of the stable boys first."

"I will."

"Let's tell this critter good night and split." Michael's voice was laced with impatience.

"What's the big hurry?" She met his gaze and chuckled.

"I . . . I just thought you might be hungry. There's a deli not far up the street that makes a mean grilled pastrami sandwich." He shrugged. "Besides, as far as I know, you haven't had anything to eat since this afternoon back at the airport."

"Thanks, but I'm still too keyed up to eat any more. I really should turn in." She gave Ebony one final pat, avoiding Michael's gaze. Though a late snack with Michael was more than tempting, she knew she mustn't. Already these few short hours with him had stirred too many confusing emotions within her.

Michael reached out and cupped her chin with his hand, gently prodding her to look at him. "Are you sure?"

"Absolutely."

"All right, then. I'll walk you to Estelle's trailer, but I doubt if she'll be there for another hour or so. She usually goes to my folks' motor home to have a bite to eat. Most likely Mom will save something for me too." He chuckled. "She always thinks if I'm left to my own culinary devices, I'll waste away."

The air was heavy with the scent of sawdust and animals, mingled with mesquite wafting from someone's small propane barbecue alongside one of the trailers.

As they started out, his arm brushed her shoulder. Though the contact was fleeting, she was acutely conscious of his nearness. A shudder rippled through her.

"Chilly?"

"Yes . . . no." She felt like a silly schoolgirl, unable to know her own mind. Though the earlier rainsqualls had been warm and humid, now the air was much too balmy to explain her physical response. How could she admit to Michael, much less to herself, that his magnetic presence was hopelessly unraveling her?

But in the wake of that awareness her memory instantly sharpened. The groupies. That showgirl. How could she ever compete — even if she did desire a relationship with Michael? No, they might as well have come from two distinct planets on the opposite sides of the galaxy. She was definitely an outsider to Michael's tightly knit world. She would remain that way no matter how long she stayed. And even if she let down her guard and allowed him to capture her in his spell, how long could it last? Would he soon move on to someone more enticing? Just as Charles had?

"Michael?"

"Hmm?"

She hesitated before going on. "Who was that showgirl you were talking to tonight?"

"Her name's Rita and she's new here. She used to be an aerialist with another circus. I hear she was pretty good. Claudette wanted me to do Rita a favor today — give her a lift — but I managed to get out of it. I went to the airport to meet you instead." He edged away

47

slightly, letting his arm drop to his side.

Lisa pushed back the fleeting thought that Michael's purpose in meeting her might've been simply to avoid giving in to his twin sister. "I bet that ticked off Claudette," she said.

"She'll get over it," he answered, his expression unreadable. "Besides, there was no reason why Claudette couldn't have played chauffeur to Rita. Rita's great-aunt Mildred — or whoever she wanted to see — apparently lives on some dude ranch near the north end of the county." They sidestepped a wardrobe trunk someone had left near the door of a fifth wheeler.

"The way I see it," Michael continued in an offhand manner, "Rita is fun to joke around with, but that's about it. If Claudette wants to buddy up with Rita that way, then fine. She doesn't need to involve me too."

Lisa shot him a questioning glance. Wasn't Michael aware of his charismatic appeal? Even something innocent like joking around might give Rita reason to believe she stood a chance with him.

"So are you trying to say Claudette's playing Cupid?" Lisa asked. "Your sister wants to bring you and Rita together?"

"Yep."

"Why?"

"It all goes back to her fear of me leaving — just like we talked about earlier. Claudette figures if I end up marrying another flyer, then I'll stay with the troupe forever."

"And what do *you* think?" She stopped walking and swung around to look at him.

"I'm going to stay, no matter what," he ground out. "I've tried it on the outside. I'm back where I belong."

"Of course. Your performance tonight made that more than obvious."

Though Michael had avoided any further references to his thoughts about marriage, his message had come through loud and clear. Michael could never make a life for himself anywhere than with the circus.

As they started walking again, a picture of Rita returned to her mind. "Any special reason why Rita decided to join Jessell and Stern?" she asked.

He chuckled. "So what's with this Rita bit? You certainly seem more than mildly interested."

"Just curious, that's all," she replied with a shrug, though she could feel her face growing warm with embarrassment. They passed two keepers carrying buckets of water.

"Rita's troupe broke up so she decided to

move on. According to Claudette, when Rita came to Jessell and Stern, she said she needed a change and wanted to work as a showgirl instead. I guess my sister's made an extra effort to welcome her."

"How accommodating," she said in a low voice. Actually, it was difficult to understand how Claudette could make *anyone* feel welcome. But maybe she wasn't being fair. Maybe she'd judged Claudette too hastily.

"What was that?"

She flushed again. "Nothing. I . . . I didn't mean that the way it probably sounded. I guess I'm more tired than I realized."

"Which means I'm doing the right thing by making sure you turn in now." He grinned again. "Not that I particularly want to, mind you."

She peered down the row of RVs. They'd almost come to the end. "Where are you staying?" she asked.

"Three doors down." He nodded to a small seventies-vintage trailer. His pickup was parked close by. "It might not be the Taj Mahal, but it gets me by."

"And Claudette? Where's her place?"

"We passed it already. Back this side of the costume trailer."

Outside Estelle's RV, Michael dug into his hip pocket and pulled out a key. "Here. Take this. It's a spare and Estelle said for you to hold onto it." He pressed the key into her palm, prolonging the contact.

"Thanks, Michael."

"Uh . . . a couple of more things. Estelle also said to tell you the bottom bunk is yours. And don't mind her little poodle. His name's Rags. Used to be one of Mom's show poodles, but Estelle's let him get soft. Anyway, he might just decide to give you an overly enthusiastic welcome. He tends to get a little carried away at times."

"Thanks again. I'll like that." She locked her gaze with his. "Sleep well, Michael."

"You too." He gave no indication of leaving, but rather leaned closer and settled his hand on the back of her neck. A suggestive smile hovered on the corners of his mouth. His lips were only a fraction away.

"Lisa?"

"Yes?"

"It's kind of weird, isn't it? I mean . . . I never expected to see you again. When I met you last year, I figured you were just another townie who wandered through."

"Well, I guess I was then. But I'm not anymore. I'm here to stay."

A shadow of doubt passed over his face. "Just hang in there, okay? Things are gonna be different here. I guarantee it."

51

"I realize that, Michael." She offered him a hesitant smile. "Truth is, I never expected to sign on with Jessell and Stern either. Serendipity, I guess. You're right. Life can be kind of weird sometimes."

"Uh-huh." *Weird and scary,* he thought. His stomach knotted. He felt as if some bozo had just kicked him in the gut. *Hold on, Figaro. Get ahold of yourself.* Yet being close to Lisa, touching her like this. . . .

His voice was ragged as he dropped his hand. "See ya . . . see you around." He hesitated, then reached for her hand and gently pressed her knuckles against his lips. "You'd better get inside. Now."

"I will."

He turned on his heel and without a backward glance strode quickly away.

She couldn't go in. She had to keep watching him. Slowly, gradually his retreating figure faded into the night. *Michael, come back!* she yearned to call to him.

No! her better judgment ruled. *You don't fit in. You could never be his. And even if you could, he'd only end up hurting you. Let him be.*

What was the matter with her? she wondered miserably as she turned the key in the lock. Why had she allowed her heart to take this crazy roller-coaster ride? And now, foolish

52

woman that she was, she wanted him more than ever.

The minute she opened the trailer door, the sound of yipping jolted her, putting a stop to her reverie.

Searching, she moved her hand against the wall edging the door frame and found what felt like a light switch, then flipped it on.

"Oh, my! Aren't you a sweetheart!"

The barking continued as she dropped to her knees and scooped the small white poodle into her arms. Rags bathed her hand in warm, wet licks. Despite herself, she had to laugh. "Do you miss Estelle? Think you can put up with another human for a while?"

Rag's smooth pink tongue moved from her hand to her chin. "My goodness! Michael was right! You really know how to make a stranger feel welcome." As she snuggled the dog close against her chest, trying to contain his squirms and wiggles, her memory skirted back to earlier that afternoon. While she and Michael had cut through the back circus lot in search of Ed Figaro, she'd noticed that several of the circus families owned pets.

In many ways, she decided, the folks who performed with Jessell and Stern appeared like any typical family — as best as she could judge from her limited experience. Here at the circus, children played kickball and hide-and-seek alongside the motor homes and trailers. When the adults weren't working, they cooked, did laundry, and talked about the weather.

Lisa set the dog back down. In a flash, Rags had scampered across the brown-carpeted floor, curled upon a beanbag chair, and squeezed his eyes shut.

Shrugging out of her windbreaker, Lisa took in the compact homeyness sur-rounding her. Posters in thin brass frames — a smiling clown, trapeze artists, and circus memorabilia from an earlier era — graced the wall behind a simple floral pat-terned couch.

At the far end of the couch lay Lisa's carry-on bag that Estelle had offered to take earlier. The small kitchenette and dining booth occupied the center of the trailer, while the bunk bed and bathroom were situ-ated on the far end.

A tangy aroma hung in the air, hinting of sautéed onions and green peppers. As Lisa looked about further, she spotted a note from Estelle on the table. *Lisa,* it read, *I hope you like chicken fajitas. There's plenty in the fridge. Help yourself to all you want — soft drinks too.*

Later, after Lisa had eaten, Estelle came inside and they climbed into their respective bunks. Though it was late and they visited only briefly, they talked almost as if they'd known each other for years. Lisa was grateful for Estelle's warm welcome. What a contrast to the way Claudette had greeted her.

"I'm sorry I'm going to have to leave earlier than usual tomorrow morning." Estelle's voice drifted from overhead. "I want to say good-bye to Papa before he has to leave. Right after that, Mom has an appointment with a poodle breeder. She wants both Claudette and me to meet him too. Fix yourself some breakfast. There's plenty of cold cereal in the cupboard above the sink."

"No problem," Lisa answered, stifling a yawn. "I'm used to taking care of myself. And thanks again for letting me stay with you," she added before saying good night. "You and me . . . we're going to make terrific roomies."

"I think so too," Estelle answered sleepily.

Lisa awoke the next morning to the beeping sound of her wristwatch alarm. What — seven already? Bolting out of bed, she squinted at the slanting sunlight that streamed in through the trailer window. Estelle had apparently taken Rags with her. The dog was nowhere in sight.

Lisa rummaged hurriedly through her overnight bag till she found the T-shirt and denim jeans she'd rolled up inside. Ed had told her to report to the veterinarian quarters — a roomy motor home that had been converted into a clinic — no later than eight.

As she was combing her hair and about to pour herself a bowl of cold cereal, a knock sounded at the door.

"Coming!" she called. She tossed the comb down and hurried to answer the door. Peering curiously outside, she spied a middle-aged man with sandy-colored hair and a deeply bronzed tan. In his hand, he clutched a brown grocery bag.

" 'Morning!"

"Good morning to you!"

"You Lisa Prentice?" he asked, squinting up at her.

"Yes!" She could hear the surprise in her voice. How did he know her when she was still a stranger to almost everyone here at Jessell and Stern?

"Pete Morehouse," he said. "I'm a rigger."

"Hello, Pete. How may I help you?" She

56

glanced discreetly at her watch, hoping he'd be brief, but at the same not wanting to appear rude. Last thing she needed was to show up late for work, especially on her first day.

"Claudette asked me to give this to you," he said, shoving the bag into her hands. "She said you'd be expectin' it."

"Why, yes! Thanks!" She was certain now that her surprise showed even more. So Claudette had come through with the extra clothing. . . . Maybe Michael's twin was sincere in wanting to help her after all.

In a flash, the man had left. Eagerly Lisa began emptying the contents of the bag onto the couch. But as the last piece of clothing tumbled out into a heap, Lisa's optimism quickly soured.

She held up the first item. Yard upon yard of fabric, its color a putrid green, emerged before her eyes. She wasn't sure what it was supposed to be, but it looked like a blouse — at least ten sizes too big! What was this? she wondered with growing disgust. Did Claudette get this stuff from clown alley? Was this some kind of a joke?

She yanked at the next article of clothing, a pair of jeans that were so badly grass-stained and smudged with ground-in dirt, there was no hope of ever salvaging them.

Most insulting of all, they looked as if they would fit one of the elephants!

Her face burned with anger. She wadded up the clothes and threw them onto the floor. "I can't believe it!" she sputtered out loud. "How can Claudette be related to Michael? His *twin*, no less!"

Blinking back tears, she spun around and headed for the door. She couldn't let anything interfere with her first assignment with Dr. Woodstock. Not even a nightmare like this!

But as she hurried across the lot, her anger mounted. She felt as if Claudette had doused her with a bucket of icy water. And a little voice deep inside of her warned that this was probably only the beginning. . . .

Chapter Four

"Where's Dr. Woodstock?" Lisa asked a young dark-skinned teenager as she poked her head into the veterinarian clinic. "I'm Lisa Prentice, his new assistant. He's meeting me here at eight." She still bristled in the wake of Claudette's cruel trick, but was determined to put her feelings aside — for the time being, at least. She was embarking on a new job. A new purpose. She mustn't let anything distract her.

"Hi. I'm Raphael. I help out wherever I'm needed." The boy, who was unloading the contents from a large cardboard box, looked up and offered a shy smile. Slender, with shiny dark hair that touched his collar, he appeared to be about fifteen. "Doc Woodstock is back at the arena," he continued. "He got called away to see what's wrong with Sudan."

"Sudan?"

"Yeah. One of the giraffes." He pierced through the thick packaging tape with his pocket knife and explained. "When it's raining hard like this, we try to find inside

59

space for the animals. Go to the south door of the arena. That'll take you right to them."

"Oh . . . all right. Thanks, Raphael."

She hurried back, following the boy's directions. The rain pattered. Sidestepping a puddle, she tugged at the hood of her windbreaker as a single raindrop slid down her cheek. She could feel her head throb with anxious anticipation. What would the day bring?

At last she found Dr. Woodstock, examining the giraffe under the uppermost section of bleachers.

"Good morning, Dr. Woodstock."

He cast her a quick glance and grunted. " 'Morning. About time you got here."

She squared her shoulders, willing herself to remain calm. Couldn't he at least say something like, "Nice to see you again," or even, "Welcome aboard?"

"I reported to the veterinarian headquarters at eight," she told him. "Just as we'd planned."

"Fine. I told Raphael to keep an eye out for you. But you'll soon discover, Miss Prentice, nothing around here goes according to plan."

"Yes, sir."

She trained her attention onto Sudan. The giraffe, who stared down at her with dark round eyes, was wedged into a large metal framework.

The veterinarian probed the animal's knee joint, manipulating it gently. "The swelling's getting worse," he muttered. "I think we'd better get a picture as soon as possible."

Fascinated, momentarily forgetting her previous uneasiness, she kept her gaze fixed on the giraffe and the strange-looking cage. She'd never seen anything like it before.

"What is that?" she asked, pointing.

"It's called a squeeze cage. The sides are built on runners so they can be brought together to hold a critter in place while I work on 'im."

Nodding, she reached out impulsively to stroke the giraffe's side. Sudan gave a start.

"Miss Prentice! You never, *ever* startle a sick animal!" he bellowed. "You, of all people, should know better than that!"

"Sorry!" Her stomach flip-flopped. She felt her muscles grow tense. *My first day on the job, and already I'm getting off to a bad start.*

The giraffe bobbed his head and turned to look at her again. He was so beautiful. Lisa hadn't meant to frighten him . . . she only wanted to touch him. But Dr. Woodstock was right. She might be inexperienced

when it came to the circus, but she understood enough about most animals to have
known better.

"Go to the clinic and get the portable X
ray," he said. His voice softened some. "You
should find it on the bottom shelf at the far
end of the trailer. And don't waste any
time."

She nodded, hoping his X-ray unit appeared similar to Doc Largent's and she
would recognize it right away. "I'll hurry,"
she promised him.

On her way, Lisa caught a glimpse of Michael, Claudette, and Estelle striding toward the main auditorium for an early-
morning practice. The sounds of their
talking and laughter drifted her way. For a
moment, she longed to be with Michael too,
instead of trying to please an already dis-
agreeable Dr. Woodstock.

Had Michael noticed her? she wondered.
If so, he'd given no indication. And what
about Claudette? Had she told the others
about her "special delivery"? Hopefully that
wasn't what they had been laughing about.

Pausing briefly, she watched them disappear through the large double doors into the
back of the auditorium. She exhaled a
wistful sigh.

When she returned with the X-ray equipment a few minutes later, Dr. Woodstock's eyebrows were raised. "Well, you didn't waste a minute finding it, now did you?" His voice held a hint of surprise.

"No, sir." Actually, Raphael had still been there and had helped her.

She handed over first the rectangular cassette that held the film, then the X-ray unit that snapped the pictures. The X ray had a cone on the top and two handles to help carry it. Without a word, he passed her the electrical cord. She struggled to plug it into the end of the extension cord that was snaked across the arena floor, but couldn't get it to fit. She kept trying, fighting back her escalating frustration. Still no luck.

"Easy," he cautioned. "Do you want to break the connection?"

"I don't understand it. Something must be bent," she stammered. She pushed the plug again. This time — what a relief — it worked!

"One of the show horses has a sinus infection," he continued evenly. "When we're done with Sudan, we must go take a look at her. Hoshi, a stable boy, told me she's not responding to the antibiotics I've given her." He positioned the cassette behind the giraffe's leg and prepared to take the first picture.

"Doc Largent always says when nothing else works, a good shot of whiskey will do the trick," she put in. She wasn't sure how receptive he'd be to Doc's old-time remedies, but figured it was worth a try anyway.

Dr. Woodstock's gaze hardened. "Thank you, Miss Prentice. But if you don't mind, I'll abide by more conventional modes of treatment."

Lisa broke out into a cold sweat. She wanted to crawl off and disappear somewhere. Anywhere. Even a squeeze cage would do.

"I hope you plan to watch me carefully and listen to everything I tell you." The veterinarian's voice pulled her back. "I don't like to waste time repeating myself." He stood back to snap the second picture, this time a side view.

"Yes, of course," she answered, tipping her chin. "And as for the horses, I'm already quite comfortable around them, you may remember. I'm so glad to hear how well Ebony's been doing this past year." Surely he hadn't already forgotten about that day back in Madison Square Garden, she thought. But in case he had, it wouldn't hurt to jog his memory a little.

He grunted again as he moved back from the giraffe. "There's more work here now

64

than three of us can handle. Obviously, I can't turn you loose working with the larger animals yet. Even the grown monkeys can be much more cantankerous than most folks realize."

She nodded agreeably and forced herself to put on a broad smile.

The rest of the day went much the same, as Lisa accompanied Dr. Woodstock from one end of the sprawling circus grounds to the other. They administered pills and injections. They hot-packed draining wounds. They splinted and set at least a half dozen fractures. They took more portable X rays. The work seemed to go on and on.

But all the time, no matter how hard she tried, Lisa couldn't seem to please him.

Late that evening, after the last show had ended, Lisa lingered wearily in the back lot, watching the work crews fly into action. Tomorrow at the crack of dawn, Jessell and Stern would be moving to the next town. Today had been one of the rare times, she'd learned, when they stayed in the same place for two days, not just one.

As she continued to look on, new fascination eclipsed her fatigue. The flurry of activity was intoxicating! Elephants trumpeted. Men shouted. Already the menagerie tent had been taken down and carted away.

Floats, riggings, and props were packed and loaded in precise order. The smells of animals mingled with the lingering scent of hot dogs and popcorn.

"Lisa!"

She jerked around. In the purple dusk, she saw Michael sauntering toward her. He was wearing a light-colored shirt that was open at the neck, a shiny dark vest, and snug-fitting jeans. Her heart leaped at the sight of him.

"I'm sorry I missed the show tonight," she said.

"I figured you were busy."

"Yes, Dr. Woodstock and I worked late. Oh, Michael, I can't begin to tell you about all those poor, sick animals. . . ."

"I know. Last spring, we traveled through some unusually damp weather." He paused, his eyes roving over her. "So what are you doing? I mean, right now?"

"Just standing here, taking it all in. I've never seen anything like this. It's incredible."

He followed her gaze. "Yep. Man and beast working together, never missing a beat," he said philosophically. "It *is* pretty amazing, isn't it?"

"Yes."

"So how did you and Doc Woodstock get

along today?" he asked, arching an eyebrow. He studied her intently as he waited for her answer.

"Good, I guess." She shrugged, then laughed nervously. "Actually, not really so good."

"Hmm." For a long moment, he held her gaze. "Well, don't let it get you down."

"I won't," she lied. "I've got big shoulders."

"Estelle and Claudette are back at the motor home," he continued. "Mom's fixing beef Stroganoff, poppy-seed noodles, and tossed green salad. She asked me to tell you you're welcome to come too. Hungry?"

"Ah . . . well." She stalled, debating how to answer. "I hate to intrude. Besides, it's awfully late." Apparently Claudette hadn't told him about what she'd done. If she had, Lisa doubted he'd be talking as if they were one big happy family.

So now what? Her thoughts raced on. Should she tell him herself? No, better not. It might make her sound like a whiner, and that certainly wasn't her style. She'd find her own way of handling this.

"Don't worry about the time," he insisted. "This is the normal dinner hour for most circus performers." He inclined his head, then broke into a lazy smile. "Actually —"

His smile broadened, showing a flash of even white teeth. "Actually, I think I have a better idea."

"Oh?"

"Let's go somewhere and grab a pizza instead. Frankly, I'm not much in the mood for beef Stroganoff right now."

"Well . . . all right. But be sure to tell your mother thanks for me. Better yet, I'll tell her myself. First chance I get tomorrow."

She met his heart-stopping gaze, privately taken aback at how quickly she'd agreed to go with him. Still, what would it hurt, this one time? She'd been running herself ragged ever since she'd arrived. She deserved an hour or so to relax. Besides, time like this alone with Michael would undoubtedly be a rarity.

"Good. So when can you be ready?"

She glanced down at her dirt-streaked jeans and soiled cotton plaid blouse and wondered when she'd ever find the time to shop for new clothes. "Oh, dear! I didn't realize I'd gotten so filthy. Give me fifteen minutes to change. I'll meet you at Estelle's trailer."

"You got it. Fifteen minutes it is." He winked, and whistling a tune, sauntered away.

Under a star-studded sky, void of further

rain, Michael swerved the pickup onto the interstate and headed east.

"You look sharp in Estelle's new tank top and jeans," he said. His eyes shone mischievously as he added, "But don't tell *her* that. She might take it as an insult." The fleeting glow of a neon light illuminated his face, then faded.

"Your sister's a lifesaver. You should see all the other stuff she's loaned me. I promised her that the first chance we got to go check out a mall, I'd treat her to anything she wants." Biting her lip, Lisa once again fought the temptation to tell him about Claudette's contribution to her wardrobe.

Off in the distance, the silhouettes of palm trees contrasted the indigo sky. Overhead, freeway signs caught the glare of their headlights. Rolling down her window, she inhaled deeply.

The night air rushed in and tousled her hair. The cool wash against her cheeks felt invigorating.

"Where are we going?" she asked.

"Estelle told me about a super pizza place she discovered when we were on tour here last year. It's not too far up the freeway."

She laughed. "If Estelle says it's good, then it's got to be."

As they drove farther away from the lights

of town, the darkness deepened. Against the horizon, the rolling contours of the treeless brown hillsides loomed. The stars grew more dazzling. Thin wisps of clouds scudded by, obscuring a waxing moon, then revealed it again.

Lisa looked about, drinking in the sights, sounds, and smells. It was so different than anything she ever experienced while living on the East Coast. Almost like magic — a summer sort of magic. Or was it because she was with Michael that her senses seemed so alive, the magic so real?

"Tired?" he asked.

"Uh-huh. But I think I'm starting to get my second wind now. And everything here's so incredibly beautiful!" She could smell the tangy fragrance wafting from a nearby orange grove. "Know something, Michael?" Smiling, she looked over at him.

"What?"

"I think I'm going to like this. Traveling from coast to coast, I mean. There's a lot of wanderlust inside of me. Surprising, I suppose, when you consider how often I changed locations during my childhood. I lived in six different states in seventeen years."

"Lisa, there's something —" He broke off.

"What's wrong, Michael?"

"Nothing. I . . . I think I see the pizza place up ahead. Estelle said we couldn't miss the sign." He turned to meet her gaze, but his expression appeared strained.

Soon they were sitting across from each other, munching slices of Canadian bacon pizza oozing with melted cheese. A small votive candle flickered in the center of the table draped by a red-and-white checkered cloth.

Scattered about the intimate café were several couples, some young, others older. In a corner booth a group of giggling teenagers waited for their order to arrive.

Michael leaned forward and reached for Lisa's hand. The flickering candlelight accented the planes and angles of his face. He appeared more handsome than ever.

For a long while, neither spoke. Then, at last, Michael broke the silence.

"Lisa. . . ."

"Yes?"

He grazed his thumb over her ring finger, studying her intently. "When we were talking earlier — about working with the circus — about the wanderlust and the travel. . . ." He hesitated.

"Go on. What is it?"

He glanced furtively about the small

71

room. *Not enough privacy,* he thought. *But I can't put it off any longer.*

"I'm concerned about you, Lisa. Sometimes I get the feeling you might have an ulterior motive. Like you might be running away."

Caution washed over her. Once again she regretted unwisely telling him about her engagement to Charles. But it was too late now. She couldn't take it back.

Shifting her weight, she feigned nonchalance. "Don't be ridiculous, Michael. That's just an old cliché about people running off with the circus. Whatever would make you say a thing like that?" She shifted beneath his steady gaze.

"The engagement, Lisa. The engagement you said came to an end. Was that why?"

She lifted one shoulder. "All right. You win. Yes, that was part of it."

"Can you talk about it? Can you tell me what happened?"

She shook her head.

The stillness stretched between them. Finally he spoke in a low voice, "I had no business asking." His eyes delved into hers as he squeezed her hand. "It . . . it wasn't fair of me."

The tension was so palpable, she could almost reach out and touch it. She let out a steadying breath. What was the use? Michael could see right through her. Besides, it was time to shoot straight with him.

"No, Michael. I'm the one who's unfair. Besides, I . . . I've held it inside for far too long." She wadded up the paper napkin she'd opened onto her lap. "His name was Charles. Charles Bergman. He was an up-and-coming lawyer in Manhattan. Climbed all the right corporate ladders. Hobnobbed with all the right people. We met at a surprise fortieth birthday party that Doc Largent threw for his wife. And . . . well, one thing sort of led to another."

"You mean it was love at first sight?"

She sipped her cola before continuing. "Yes — at least as far as I was concerned. Before I realized it, I was completely taken by him. It wasn't long before I believed he loved me also." She pursed her lips, blinking back a tear. "But then, why shouldn't I have? He gave me an engagement ring, swore there'd never be another. But . . . but then one day he announced it was over. He said we weren't compatible, that I'd never understand the demands of his profession. He also . . . told me he'd fallen in love with a district attorney. Her name was Ramona. Ramona Fullerton. Anyway . . . Charles said they planned to marry soon . . . on Valentine's Day." His face became a watery blur as a finally released tear coursed down her cheek. "It all happened so fast."

He let go of her hand, and with infinite tenderness, brushed the tear away. "Ah, Lisa. What a fool Charles was. What a fool to let you go."

She couldn't remove her gaze from his. His eyes, those deep blue pools, brimmed with understanding.

Yet she felt suddenly exposed. Exposed and vulnerable. Pulling herself from her spiraling thoughts, she forced her attention back to what he was saying.

"There's something I want to tell you, Lisa." He took her hand again and squeezed it harder. "Will you hear me out?"

"Of course. What is it?"

"After a while the highways — the towns — well, they all start to look the same. You've got to love the circus because it's become a part of you. You've got to breathe it. Eat it. Make it your own. For me, being an aerialist is who I am — not just what I do."

"I *do* want that," she said. "More than anything in the world. Please believe me, my motivations involve more than just running. Working with the circus means the world to me too, Michael. Besides, I'm a survivor. I intend to give it whatever it takes."

He didn't appear convinced. He took another bite of pizza, and chewed slowly. "Perhaps. I know we've already talked about it briefly, Lisa, but you might be up against more than you realize. Doc's first assistant lasted only three weeks. The second managed to hang on till only two weeks before her probation period was up, then threw in the towel and left anyway."

Visions of Claudette flashed through her mind. Hadn't Michael's twin issued subtle warnings too — her own hidden agenda? Unexpectedly Lisa's anger flared. Why was everyone trying to discourage her? Or more to the point, trying to drive her away? Why, now, Michael too?

"I'm not sure where this conversation is leading us, Michael," she said tightly, "but now it's my turn to speak." Her head throbbed. "Maybe you think I'm not going to make it with Jessell and Stern, but you're wrong. Dead wrong! I'm not sure why it should even matter to you. And if it should turn out that I become assistant number three who goes down the tubes, it's *my* life! And I'll be darned if I'm going to let another man step in again and try to ruin it!"

There! She'd said it. Fighting back another flood of tears, she sprang to her feet and marched toward the restaurant door.

"Lisa! Wait! I didn't mean it that way! I . . . I was only trying to help." Michael sprinted after her.

Alongside the pickup, she stopped in her tracks. He planted both hands firmly on her shoulders, waiting for her to face him. "Lisa, I'm sorry. Really I am. I don't want to fight."

She couldn't let him see the tears streaming down her face. With much effort, she choked back a sob.

"Lisa. Look at me. Please."

Hesitantly she turned around and lifted her gaze. The expression on his face made fresh tears fall.

Wordlessly he reached out again to brush them away. His touch was driving her insane.

"Oh, Michael. I'm sorry too. I must . . . I must be more tired than I realized." She toyed with the collar of his lightweight jacket and offered him a contrite smile. "Please forgive me?"

How could she excuse herself? Explain to him that Claudette's cruel trick had left her a trifle suspicious and a lot afraid? She had no recourse. She couldn't let him know. She'd already determined to handle it alone, and she wouldn't back down.

"Let's just forget it," Michael said hoarsely, pulling her closer. His mouth covered hers. Softly at first, then with unexpected urgency.

She leaned into him, kissed him back, immersing herself in his tempting nearness. The kiss deepened.

Foolishly her emotions carried her away. Yes, it had to be magic. Not merely the night sounds, the moonlight, nor the stars tracking the heavens.

The magic was Michael.

Chapter Five

The first part of July arrived, hot and sultry. The circus had journeyed farther south, then crossed Texas through wide-open spaces dotted with cattle ranches and rolling plains that gave way to mountains and pine forests.

Time alone with Michael had been limited, just as he'd forewarned. Many nights after the last show, Lisa met him at the stabling quarters where she helped him feed, exercise, and groom the horses. On a few occasions, they'd fixed a simple late-night meal inside his trailer, or ate with Mrs. Figaro in the motor home.

But early each morning when they continued their travels, she rode with Estelle — not Michael. Somehow, she'd sensed that arrangement suited Michael too.

Then there were her twelve-hour work days, one calamity after another. As each day wore on, she found herself closer to the brink of exhaustion.

One morning, she'd forgotten to check the latch on a cage. Three feisty chimps escaped and took refuge atop a palm tree. To make matters worse, these chimps were the star performers in a highly publicized clown act and the show was starting in less than an hour.

The keepers and Lisa tried everything imaginable to get the chimps down. Nothing worked. The clowns were upset, making Lisa even more flustered. Dr. Woodstock only stood by wordlessly, shaking his head with disgust. Finally, a mere five minutes before curtain time, one of the riggers emerged on the scene with a tall extension ladder.

"Everyone stand back," he'd ordered. "I'll take care of it."

Take care of it, he did. He captured the chimps. But they were still so riled up after their escape, the clown couldn't get them to cooperate and the act was a big flop. All because of Lisa.

Yesterday had turned out equally disastrous. Forgetting that camels have a predisposition for spitting, she'd let her guard slip. While she was helping Dr. Woodstock pour medicine down a camel's throat, the animal got upset and started spitting. The vet managed to duck clear in the nick of time, but not Lisa. Before she realized what had happened, she was half covered with the most horrid-smelling acid liquid.

Today Jessell and Stern was set up in a vacant lot not far from Galveston.

"Miss Prentice, get a move on!" Dr. Woodstock barked the minute she'd reported to the clinic. "We need to examine the elephants. Go fetch the treatment cart. The smaller one will do."

"Right away, Dr. Woodstock." She wished he would call her Lisa instead. That might take the edge off their professional relationship. Doc Largent had always called her by her first name, but of course, he'd been not only her boss, but a good friend too.

The cart, which was sandwiched between a metal file cabinet and small bookcase, had two shelves with compartments for first aid supplies. Quickly she retrieved it and steered it down the ramp that angled off the front steps of the motor home/clinic.

"Several elephants have foot problems," Dr. Woodstock said in his usual no-nonsense way as he trailed close behind her. "Walter, the elephant trainer, will be helping us. Your job is to hand me the medication and make note of it in the records." He paused, narrowing his dark brown eyes on her. "Elephants can be extremely dangerous. But Walter's the best. He knows exactly how to handle them."

She nodded, trying to swallow the lump in her throat. *Yes, Walter,* she thought. She dreaded facing him. Michael had been right. He and the other trainers had taken a dim view of her. More than once she'd overheard Walter referring to her as unskilled and clumsy when he was talking with the other animal trainers.

Maybe she *was* nothing more than an amateur, she told herself dolefully. Maybe they were right. But no, she mustn't believe that, no matter how discouraged she became. She couldn't let her confidence wane.

Dr. Woodstock must have sensed her misgivings, because over the rattle of the treatment cart, his voice grew less gruff. "Don't worry about the elephants, Miss Prentice. They seldom suffer from a major illness. They usually have small things go wrong."

"Like what?"

"Mostly foot infections and sore cuticles. I have the keepers tend to the daily treatments. But once every week, in order to assess their overall condition, I do it myself."

As they drew nearer, she spied Walter. Tall and bronze-skinned, he was talking to one of the massive creatures. Each was chained to a ring in the ground by one front foot and one hind leg.

Walter held a stick about the size of a

broom handle. He called it an elephant hook, explaining that elephants and their assistants use it to gently prod the huge animals into following directions.

"Thatta girl, Rosy," Walter said in a firm voice. "Good Rosy."

The elephants were lined up like mammoth beady-eyed soldiers standing very close together, Rosy up front. Their massive gray bulk fascinated Lisa.

"Is something wrong with Rosy's trunk?" she asked the veterinarian. "She's not moving it like the others are."

"Her trunk's paralyzed," he answered. "Still, she's learned to compensate. As you can see, she manages to feed herself by throwing back her head and catching her food in midair."

"That's amazing," Lisa said. She pulled back the white towel that covered the treatment cart and took a quick inventory. Yes, it was all there, everything from the assorted bottles, vials, and syringes, to the scissors, gauze dressings, and other odds and ends.

Immediately they set to work. Using the hook, Walter nudged Rosy to lift her foot while Dr. Woodstock examined it.

"Doesn't the hook hurt them?" she asked. She was taking a chance by asking, she knew. Walter might take her question as a personal affront. But she was concerned for the elephants. She had to know.

"Not at all, miss," the trainer answered agreeably. "The hook —" he nodded to the curved piece of metal on the end of the stick "— it's quite dull, really. It simply lets the elephant know what I expect it to do."

As they worked, unexpected satisfaction filled her. What had caused this turnaround? She and the two men were actually carrying on a congenial conversation. Moreover, Dr. Woodstock was treating her as a colleague. Even Walter seemed to respect her.

Rosy passed the foot inspection successfully. But when they came to the second elephant, Dr. Woodstock noticed a badly inflamed cuticle that was oozing pus. "Hand me that bottle with the spray top," he told Lisa. "Next I'll need the Silvadene ointment."

"Right here," Lisa answered efficiently as she opened a large plastic jar and passed it to him. They continued in that manner, moving from one elephant to the next. Finally they came to the end of the line. The last two elephants, Mildred and Bessie, were younger than the rest. Lisa remembered Estelle telling her they'd come recently to the circus all the way from Indonesia. With rapt attentiveness, Lisa watched them trunking up and munching a fresh supply of timothy hay.

Dr. Woodstock shook his head as he probed Bessie's front foot with a gloved hand. "For crying out loud, Bessie, when are we ever going to get that sore healed? And Walter, we simply must find time to shorten Bessie and Mildred's tusks. We've put it off far too long."

"You're right, Doc," he replied. "How about today after the matinee?"

"Good idea. Let's plan on it."

"Why do you shorten their tusks?" Lisa asked. The vet pointed to a gauze pad on the treatment cart before answering. Deftly she handed it to him.

"We perform that simple operation to make the elephants less dangerous to work with," he explained. "Usually it's done as soon as they come into the circus, but as you know, time has been scarce lately."

"Also, elephants sometimes break their tusks," Walter pointed out. "So shortening them makes good sense for two reasons."

"Do you have to give them any anesthetic?" she asked him.

"Not under usual circumstances. A lot of people don't realize that elephants don't have any feeling in their tusks. All we normally use is a simple hacksaw."

She peered again at the young elephants and smiled. They were adorable with their small pink mouths and glittering dark eyes.

"Miss Prentice, hand me the Coppertox," Dr. Woodstock said.

She reached for the bottle, gripping the spray-top handle. A stream of liquid shot out, barely missing the top of her head. Instantly she released her grip. The liquid kept spurting. What was wrong? she wondered frantically. Why didn't it stop? By now half the stuff on the treatment cart was soaked!

"I can't believe this!" Lisa cried. "The release valve must be stuck!"

"For crying out loud, give me that bottle," Dr. Woodstock fumed. "*I'll* fix it."

She moved toward him, stumbled, and fell hard against the cart, dropping the spray bottle. The cart crashed to the ground. The medical supplies scattered. Then a brown jug flipped on its side and started rolling directly toward Bessie.

In one quick motion, the elephant bobbed her head, let out an ear-shattering squeal, and lunged forward. The vet and trainer sprang out of her way.

Lisa cringed, squeezing her eyes shut. The sound of Bessie's tusk as it struck a large metal drum thundered in her ear.

Slowly she forced open her eyes. She blinked, paralyzed with disbelief. There on the ground next to the emptied spray bottle lay Bessy's broken-off tusk.

Silence. An eternity of silence. At least Bessie had calmed down.

Gathering her courage, Lisa finally looked at Dr. Woodstock. The artery in his neck throbbed. His face was crimson with anger.

"Miss Prentice!"

"I'm sorry," she gasped. Tears prickled her eyes, but she blinked them back. No. She absolutely would not let them see her cry.

"I've already told you the first day you came, you never startle the animals!"

"That's right!" Walter jumped in. His voice trembled with controlled anger. His eyes flashed. "You could've gotten us all killed!"

"I'm sorry," she stammered again, willing her hands to stop shaking. "It was an accident. I . . . I don't know why that spray bottle got stuck."

The vet sent her a cold, hard glare, then rolled up his sleeves. "Well, Walter. Let's get to work. Bessie's tusks will have to be shortened. There's no point in waiting any longer."

★ ★ ★

Late that night in an open field that joined the circus grounds, Lisa rode Ebony. They were galloping at full speed, just as the day's events continued to gallop through her mind. She yearned to be alone, to unravel her frenzied thoughts. Right now not even Michael could comfort her. All she needed were peace and solitude — plus one special horse.

Happy sounds drifted from the auditorium, contrasting with her melancholy. The last minutes of the evening show. The applause from the crowds. The roll of drums. The explosion of sound from the marching band.

As they started galloping around the next loop, a swirl of dust rose, a chalky billow in the gray twilight. *What if Michael's right?* she wondered as the clopping of Ebony's hoofbeat faded into her thoughts. *What if I'm forced to leave? What if I can't pass my probation? I'm already halfway through. Can I redeem myself in the remaining four weeks?*

Michael. The thought of him twisted her heart. She couldn't face him now. Most likely, he'd already heard what had happened. She was certain everyone at Jessell and Stern had heard.

As they slowed to a canter, she breathed in

the tangy smells of salt water. The beach wasn't far away, she remembered. The ribbon of highway they'd traveled early that morning had paralleled the coastline's lengthy expanse — miles and miles of white sand stretching along the Gulf of Mexico.

What she'd give to be there now. Away from Dr. Woodstock and the trainers. Away from the circus. Away from her problems.

Even away from Michael.

A movement in the shadows caught her attention, making her look up. Michael was sprinting toward her. She felt the color drain from her face. "Why didn't you let anyone know where you were taking Ebony?" he asked, relief filling his voice.

"I told Estelle. She must've forgotten."

"Oh. Maybe she did." In the purple darkness, she could feel him regarding her earnestly. "Are . . . are you all right, Lisa?"

"Yes. Just exhausted." She jerked her eyes away, her voice hushed. "I suppose you heard."

"Uh-huh." He paused. "Come on. Get down. Let's take Ebony back to the horses' tent."

Without protest, Lisa dismounted and, gripping the halter, started walking. "I . . . I needed to get away by myself with Ebony," she explained half apologetically. "I needed to think things through." The rustle of the parched field grass beneath their feet melded with the sound of their voices.

"Do you want to talk about it?"

"No. I'm fine now." She avoided looking at him. If she did, he'd surely read it in her eyes. He'd know she was lying.

They sidestepped a large rock, then came to the gate. "Listen, Lisa. Even if you don't need to talk, there's something I have to say."

"What?"

"Don't beat yourself up. Everyone learns by their mistakes."

"But Walter was right! I could've gotten us all killed!" Her head still throbbed as she recalled his outburst of anger.

"All right. But now you've learned. And as far as the broken tusk goes, Doc and Walter were going to shorten it anyway. Besides —" his voice softened "— it wasn't your fault that bottle went crazy and you knocked over the treatment cart."

"No point making up excuses, Michael," she insisted. "I'm sure Dr. Woodstock's still so upset with me, he doesn't see it that way."

"Sure, he's a perfectionist, but he's not totally unreasonable."

"Well, that may be." She sniffled. "But I still wouldn't blame him if he fired me first thing tomorrow." *Be grateful,* a little voice in-

89

side her spoke. *At least Michael's not saying "I told you so."*

"Speaking of tomorrow," he said, pushing open the gate. Ebony let out a snort and whinnied. "We have a day off. It's a holiday, you know."

"A holiday?" One day had blurred into the next. She'd nearly forgotten about the Fourth of July.

"Absolutely. No travel. No shows. Sometimes we perform on the Fourth, but this year we negotiated not to." They arrived at the first of several horses' tents. The familiar shouts of the stable boys and the smells of sawdust and animals wafted on the night air. "I've even promised myself for twenty-four hours, I'll forget about practicing," he added.

"Really, Michael?" She laughed softly, feeling a little better. "You sure you can handle all that free time?" she teased.

"Absolutely."

"So what are you going to do?" she asked, looking up at him.

A smile lifted one corner of his mouth. "Maybe you should be asking what *we're* going to do."

"Oh?"

"I'm taking you to Galveston. Right now you need a break more than I do."

90

He was right. She did need a break, a chance to clear her head — but certainly not with him. He was much too enticing, too wonderful in every way. She opened her mouth to turn him down, but the eagerness in his voice cut her off.

"Let's do some sight-seeing, Lisa. Check out the shops and the Historic Railroad Museum. Or if you'd rather, maybe we could pack a big picnic lunch with lots of junk food, head for the beach, and spend the day lying in the sun."

"But maybe Dr. Woodstock won't let me." It was a logical excuse, the first to spring to her mind. "You know how over-worked we are right now," she reminded him.

He shrugged. "Everyone else will be getting the time off. Why shouldn't you? Besides, I'm sure it's written in your contract."

"I don't know, Michael. Give me a while. I'll have to think about it."

He shrugged. "Suit yourself."

They proceeded to tie up Ebony and give her fresh water and hay. Then they started for the far end of the lot where the trucks and trailers were parked. As they ambled along, approaching the Figaros' motor home, he cupped his hand against the back of her neck. His touch warmed her, chipping away at her resolve.

In her peripheral vision, she thought she spied movement through the RV window. Squinting, she peered harder just as a human-shaped shadow faded away.

"So what do you say?" he asked again, his eagerness resurfacing. "Will you say yes about tomorrow? Will you go with me to Galveston?"

She stopped to face him, and again wrestled with her misgivings. Her heart was winning out. "Okay, Michael. But only on two conditions."

"What?"

"First, I want to make sure Dr. Woodstock hasn't any objections. Second, a lot will also depend on the animals. I'll go only if there are no emergencies."

"You won't be sorry, Lisa. Besides, Doc Woodstock can work alone now and then. He's done it before."

She released a slow, steadying breath. One day with Michael. For one precious day she could forget her troubles and have Michael Figaro all to herself — away from the showgirls, away from the groupies, away from the responsibilities and schedules. The thought tugged at her, causing her heart to beat faster, filling her with unexplainable pleasure.

A door from the motor home creaked open, then slammed shut.

"Hi."

"Hi, Claudette." Michael grinned openly at her.

Lisa held her breath. Had it been Claudette watching them? In a flash her thoughts rolled back to that first morning when she'd been alone in Estelle's trailer — the horrid green fabric, the humongous soiled jeans. Every time she'd come across them, she'd resolved to throw them away. For some reason, though, she never had.

"Guess what, Michael?" Claudette drawled. She lifted a shoulder and flashed him a coy smile. "The only thing I have to do tomorrow on our day off is have a friendly little chat with Doc Woodstock. Then I'm as free as a bird."

Chat with Dr. Woodstock? What about? Lisa wondered in horror. Would Claudette convince him to fire her before Lisa's probation was up?

"Lisa and I have been talking about our day off too," Michael replied amicably. "We've already decided what we're going to do."

"You have?"

"Uh-huh. We're going to drive to Galveston. Spend the entire day kicking around."

93

Claudette clasped her hands together in a gesture of eagerness. "Oh, Michael. What a terrific idea! Why didn't I think of that?" She paused, her smile growing wider, a strange glint springing to her eyes. "Can Rita and I come with you too?"

Chapter Six

"Gosh, Claudette. That's a stupid thing to ask," Michael answered between clenched teeth. "Lisa and I need time alone." *There she goes again,* he thought glumly. *Trying to set me up with Rita. Well, she'd better not try to interfere this time, because I won't let her. There's too much at stake. If Lisa's not careful, she's gonna stress out for sure.*

"Now don't get your hackles up," Claudette said. "I . . . I just thought it might be a cozy foursome, that's all." She lowered her gaze, exposing a dark fringe of eyelashes against maddeningly flawless skin. "After all, Galveston's a great big city. Rita and I might need a little extra help finding our way around."

"Oh, come off it, Claudette! You expect me to believe that?"

"Some brother you are! You're impossible." She threw up her hands in defeat and sighed. Then she turned on her heel and stepped back inside the motor home. "Sorry I asked, Michael. Good night, all."

The morning dawned bright and sunny

with the promise of clear skies. What perfect weather for a holiday, Lisa thought as she hurried to get dressed. She reached inside the closet for a red, white, and blue T-shirt with a star in the middle and a sporty pair of red slacks.

Back near Phoenix, Arizona, she and Estelle had managed a quick trip to a shopping mall off the interstate. Lisa had not only purchased several outfits, but two new pieces of luggage to store them in. Extra closet space was sorely limited in Estelle's small trailer.

Now they were breakfasting together, savoring golden-crusted waffles and fresh sliced strawberries topped with whipped cream. Rags, having lapped up the remainder of the cream, was taking a snooze, nestled into Estelle's beanbag chair.

"I love your dishes," Lisa said softly, running a finger around the rim of a white porcelain dinner plate decorated in delicate patterns of blue forget-me-nots. She swallowed against the lump in her throat, remembering her own set of blue-and-white dishes she'd donated to charity, plus all the other treasures she'd left behind.

She missed Doc Largent and her friends too — especially Melinda. Had uprooting herself to begin a new life here really been worth it?

"I know it might seem silly, using my good china for everyday, but sometimes I do it anyway," Estelle said. Lifting a matching coffee server, she filled first Lisa's cup, then her own. The aroma of the rich, strong brew wafted about them.

"Have you heard anything from your father lately?" Lisa asked. "Is he going to come back soon?"

A small frown line bridged Estelle's delicately arched eyebrows. "Mother phoned Papa yesterday just as he'd arrived back from another meeting with Uncle Peter's lawyer. He thinks more than ever now he'll be gone till the end of the summer. He kept reminding my mother to tell Michael to keep a close eye on Ebony." She shook her head and smiled, a distant look shining in her eyes. "Papa's sure crazy about that horse."

"I am too," Lisa said.

"Yes, I know. We all are." Estelle paused. "So what are you going to do today?"

Lisa told her, purposefully avoiding the part about Claudette's plea to include Rita and herself. Though Lisa was tempted to let Estelle know everything about Claudette, she kept quiet. If circus families were as close-knit as Michael had confirmed, it wouldn't be a smart move on her part.

"Mom and I talked about taking in a dog show later this morning at the fairgrounds up the road," Estelle said with a quick smile. "Then later tonight we might watch some of the fireworks that the younger kids and their parents will be setting off."

"You don't mind? Sticking around here?" Lisa asked. She was still thinking about Claudette.

"Of course not. I've been to Galveston plenty of times before. So have Michael and Claudette."

Pursing her lips, Lisa nodded without comment. Estelle's remark had only confirmed her suspicions. Claudette didn't need Michael's help getting around Galveston any more than the President needed help finding his way back to the White House.

Estelle eyed Lisa thoughtfully before going on. "So you and my brother are starting to see each other?"

"Uh . . . no, not really. As you know, there isn't much time to socialize." Lisa avoided Estelle's steady gaze as she stared down at the pat of melted butter on her half-eaten waffle.

"But what about today? Wouldn't you call this a date?"

"Michael is just concerned. He thinks I need to get away for a while."

"He has good reason to be concerned," Estelle said, wiping the corner of her mouth with a white paper napkin. "I mean, people sometimes get the wrong idea, you know? They come to the shows, see all the sequins, lights, and glitter, and think our life is just one big glamorous night after another."

"But I'm not one of those people, Estelle. I do know the difference."

"Most likely you do. But knowing and experiencing can be two different things."

"Well, as far as Michael and I seeing each other, it's all in the best interest of furthering my career. He's treating me like a sister, just like he treats you —" she faltered "— and I guess Claudette too." Lisa struggled to wipe out the memory of his kisses, and felt a slow flush rise from her neck to her cheeks. Could Estelle guess she was bending the truth?

Estelle stared at her coffee mug, toying with the handle. "You're right, Lisa. My brother cares about what happens to you here. But I also think he cares in another way."

"Oh? What do you mean?" Estelle's words caught Lisa by surprise.

"Ever since that day he met you in Madison Square Garden, he's never stopped talking about you. In fact, when he quit the troupe to strike out on his own, Claudette was convinced his real reason was to go look for you."

Lisa felt light-headed, as if she couldn't get enough air. Michael hadn't stopped talking about her? A swirl of mixed emotions swept over her. Elation . . . confusion . . . mostly, fear. But what was it she feared the most? Michael himself, or the way he was affecting her?

"But obviously Claudette was wrong," Lisa said, swishing a hand through the air. "At the time, I was just someone else for Michael to flirt with. Actually, I never heard from your brother again. It was sheer coincidence I ended up back here."

"I'm sure, though, if he hadn't been so intent on finding himself, discovering what it was he really wanted to do, he would've tracked you down."

"And now Michael is equally single-minded," Lisa insisted, though inside she was still quaking. "He knows he'll be a flyer forever. He seems to think I'm going to leave the circus, either by my own choice or because I have to — which after what happened yesterday could be more true than I'd like to admit." She gave an exaggerated shrug. "So why on earth would Michael

100

want to get involved with someone he might never see again?"

Now it was Estelle's turn to nod without comment. Yet the look in her eyes told Lisa she didn't buy it.

"All right, all right." Lisa backed down. "I'll admit, maybe Michael's interest in me might be a little more than that of a brother. And I'll also admit, I'm attracted to him too. But that's where it ends, Estelle. It's nothing more than physical attraction. Truth is, I don't want a romantic commitment either."

Over a second round of waffles, she haltingly explained about her broken engagement.

"Michael's not like Charles," Estelle said softly after Lisa had finished her story. "Even though there's probably a million women out there who'd love to get to know Michael, and he *can* be a hopeless flirt at times, he would never stray." She sighed, flashing Lisa a wistful smile. "I just hope that when I find the love of my life, it'll be someone wonderful like my brother."

A loud rap at the trailer door interrupted their conversation. "Sis! Lisa! You still there?"

Lisa glanced at her watch. What was Michael doing here so early?

Rags barked.

"Door's unlocked!" Estelle called. "Come in, Michael."

Flustered, Lisa sprang up from her seat. Had he overheard what she and Estelle had been talking about?

" 'Morning, Lisa. Sis." As he stepped inside, his masculine physique seemed to fill the doorway. He wore off-white khaki slacks and a light blue open-collared shirt with the sleeves cuffed up.

Michael broke into a dazzling smile, his eyes fixed on Lisa. "Wow! You look terrific! Where'd you get that outfit?"

She returned his smile. "Quick shopping trip. Estelle helped me. I've been saving it for something special." Lisa's heart raced.

"My sister has good taste, eh?" He shoved his hands into his hip pockets and rocked back on his heels.

Lisa's gaze dropped from Michael's suntanned face to a thin gold chain encircling his neck. The sunlight, slanting through the trailer window, touched it, causing it to glimmer.

"I . . . I hope I'm not interrupting anything," he went on as he looked first at Estelle, then Lisa.

"No, of course not," Estelle got to her feet also.

"Good." He cleared his throat. "So, Lisa. Ready to go?"

"Yes. Just give me a minute or two to help Estelle clean up here." She began collecting the dishes with more flourish than necessary.

"Oh, Lisa! Don't bother. I'll take care of this." Estelle's eyes shone with eagerness as she hurriedly waved them off.

Galveston. A city of romance. Everywhere Lisa and Michael turned, there was a multitude of enchanting sights and sounds — the huge five-acre railroad museum, a restored merchant sailing ship, the Grand Opera House, and mile after mile of sandy beaches surrounding the island city.

Later they sat atop a horse-drawn tram that toured the east end of town. As they clopped along past stately old Victorian homes and perfectly manicured front yards, the sun shone hot against their backs. The sweet smells of tropical flowers drifted on a gentle breeze.

"This is wonderful," Lisa told Michael with a sigh, leaning her head on his shoulder. "Already I'm beginning to feel so relaxed." His nearness. His smile. His gentle laughter. Yes, the magic was flowing through her again, this time more vividly than ever.

He nuzzled her hair with the tip of his chin, his hand grazing her cheek. "Just what the doctor ordered," he murmured, turning her to him. "A day in the sunshine. Sealed with a kiss."

In the space of a heartbeat, his lips brushed hers with an unfathomable tenderness that made shivers of delight ripple through her. He pulled her nearer, holding her gently against him while he deepened the kiss. Then with obvious restraint, Michael broke the contact and eased back.

"Thank you, Michael," Lisa murmured.

"Thanks for the kiss?" he teased, tossing her a devilish grin.

"No, silly." She poked him playfully in the ribs. "Thanks for bringing me here today. You were right. This is exactly what I needed."

The tram swayed from side to side with the rhythm of the horses' clopping. A car revved its engine. From farther away, a police siren shrilled, rose to full pitch, then faded away.

Michael stretched, then asked, "When we're done with our tour, you still want to head over to the beach?"

"Oh, yes! Let's do that." Her eyes strayed

to a group of people standing on the corner. Recognition gripped her. Her stomach turned over. "Oh, no. . . ." she groaned, nudging Michael in the side.

"What's the matter?"

"I think . . . I think I see Claudette. And Rita." She jerked her head in their direction. "There with those other people."

Michael frowned as he followed her gaze. "So it looks like they came anyway," he said under his breath. "Taking a little tour of their own." His tone sharpened. "Hopefully a *walking* tour."

The tram slowed to a halt not far from where they were standing. To Lisa's horror, Claudette and Rita clambered aboard. They reminded her of Christmas shoppers as they threaded their way to the back, arms laden with an assortment of packages.

"Room for us too?" Claudette asked without preamble. Before Michael could answer, they plopped down in the opposite seat.

Lisa felt her blood run cold. She couldn't believe Claudette had had the nerve to ignore what Michael had told her. Sidling up closer to Michael, Lisa longed to recapture the magic they'd shared only moments earlier. Yet she couldn't. Already the spell had been broken, the magic snatched away.

Michael slanted his twin a disapproving look. "I thought I told you that Lisa and I wanted this day to ourselves."

"Oh, for heaven's sake, Michael." Claudette wore an innocent smile. "Since when have you ever cut me out of your plans?"

"Probably not soon enough," he muttered. "I hope you two are planning to get off at the next stop."

"Are you kidding?" Claudette exclaimed. "This tour is costing us a pretty penny, and Rita and I intend to get our money's worth." She paused, wrinkling her elegant nose. "Besides, I'm done riding those horrible old buses. And my feet are killing me."

"Yeah, the last bus made Claudette carsick," Rita explained.

"I didn't realize you're prone to motion sickness," Michael said to Claudette. The anger in his voice turned to concern.

"Oh, it's nothing," Claudette insisted. "Nothing more, I'm sure, than those horrid exhaust fumes." She juggled her packages, dropping a sheet of paper.

Michael reached down to retrieve it. "What's this?"

"A flyer. We got it at a tourist information center," Rita quickly supplied. "It tells about all the stuff going on in Galveston this summer." She tossed her shoulder-length auburn hair and added, "So what y'all been up to?"

"Sight-seeing," Michael answered, his voice level. He turned the flyer over, scanned it, then without comment handed it back to Claudette.

"We've been hitting the antique shops and jewelry stores," Rita said. She turned to Michael and flashed him a resplendent smile. Rummaging through her shopping bags, she fished out a small white box, then popped it open. "Isn't this lovely, Michael?"

He peered at a large emerald ring inside and smiled back. "Yes. Very nice."

The tram lunged forward and they were once again clopping along. They rounded the corner past an old stone church. A young couple with two whining kids in tow stopped to gawk.

"Are you planning to see the fireworks display on the beach tonight?" Claudette asked. Her gaze flicked momentarily onto Lisa, then back to Michael. "Or are you two gonna make your own sparks fly?"

Lisa's face burned. She had all she could do to keep tossing back an insulting reply.

"Claudette! That's entirely uncalled for," Michael said icily.

"Pardon me." Claudette tipped her chin,

apparently unrebuffed. "Well, whatever you do, Michael, I just hope you save some time for the Fourth of July street dance on the Strand tonight."

"Where's the Strand?" he asked.

"That's the National Historic Landmark District downtown," Rita answered for Claudette.

"Oh, yeah . . . now I remember." Michael's eyes sought Lisa's as if silently asking whether she'd like to go.

"So meet us on the Strand about eight-thirty," Rita prompted. "It's going to be fabulous. The band's the best around. I'm even acquainted with the drummer, a guy named Danny Holcomb."

"Rita, how do you know so much about Galveston?" Lisa asked, hoping to divert the conversation. Without a doubt, trouble was brewing. Try as she might, she couldn't blot out the memory of Rita lingering by Michael's dressing room that first night she'd arrived.

"I was born and raised not far from here," Rita replied. "My daddy's the manager of a big condo complex next to the beach. I thought Claudette already told y'all." Her lips lifted in a pouty smile.

"No, she didn't," Michael answered cautiously. "She said you'd both be like lost

sheep trying to find your way around —
though of course she's visited this city as
many times as I."

Claudette's face matched her ruby-red
lipstick. She averted her gaze onto the landscape passing by, fanning herself with the
flyer and saying nothing.

"Oh, that silly sister of yours," Rita said,
as if Claudette had somehow suddenly disappeared. "How could she have forgotten
about my daddy? We're such good friends
now, I swear she knows everything about
me."

Claudette looked pointedly at Michael.
"Hold on, everyone. Somehow we seem to
be getting off the subject. A couple of minutes ago, Michael, I asked if you and Lisa
would like to meet us at the street dance.
You still haven't answered me."

"Well . . ." Michael shrugged. "Maybe. I
can't remember the last time I got to go to a
dance." He looked expectantly at Lisa
again, allowing his thoughts to take flight.
He could imagine her in his arms, all soft
and feminine, swaying to the beat of the
music, her petite body pressed close to his.
So why not? Besides, the place would most
likely be packed. He and Lisa would have
little problem ditching Claudette and Rita.

"What do you say, Lisa?" he asked, his

gaze still fixed on her.

She read the eagerness in his eyes. Clearly Michael wanted to go. How could she say no? After all, this was his holiday too. She had to admit, dancing under the moon and stars did sound romantic. And Michael probably already had a plan in mind to keep his twin sister from trying to bamboozle him.

Lisa shrugged too. "Sounds okay to me."

Claudette beamed.

Rita also appeared pleased.

The sound of Rita's voice sliced through Lisa's reverie. "Be sure to bring lightweight jackets. It might get chilly. By the way, I just know you'll love the band. Cloudburst, they're called — a local group. Danny used to sit behind me in the fifth grade. Even then he liked to beat out a bongo rap on his desk."

She heaved a sigh before babbling on. "Anyway, here I am again in good old Galveston after such a long time. I must confess, though, I feel more like a tourist than a native Texan. At least Claudette and I won't have to go back to the circus grounds tonight. We're staying at my daddy's."

"Tell me about the first circus you traveled with," Michael said to Rita with obvious interest. "Was it as good as Jessell and Stern?"

Lisa pushed back her annoyance and forced herself to smile at him. Was he simply being polite to Rita? Or was he flirting again?

Unbidden, jealousy gnawed at her. Maybe she shouldn't have agreed so readily to go to the dance. Obviously Estelle believed Michael was a one-woman man, but how well did she really know her brother?

"Oh yes, the first circus. Holman and Company, they called themselves." Rita smiled coyly at him through half-lidded eyes. "I'm not sure why I wasted so much time with that little dog and pony show. But at least I got to try my hand at flying. And I'd love nothing more than to have the chance to get back into it again."

"And that time may be coming sooner than we think," Claudette blurted out. Averting her gaze, she scrunched down in her seat.

"Oh, yeah?" Michael's interest was full-blown. "What do you mean, Sis?"

Her eyes darted between Michael and Lisa. "I . . . I mean . . . someday, who knows? One of us may decide to call it quits. Or expand our act." She shrugged. "Use four flyers instead of three."

One of us may call it quits. Lisa went rigid as the anger churned up inside of her. So

Claudette still believed she was trying to snatch Michael away. Without a doubt, that hurriedly added comment about expanding their act was merely a cover.

Lisa bit down on her lower lip, her thoughts spinning as she averted her gaze. Yes, Claudette's hidden message had come through loud and clear. What was she scheming to do next?

Chapter Seven

As Lisa and Michael danced cheek-to-cheek to a country golden oldie, the music wove about them like lush, velvet ribbons.

The lead singer's rich tenor voice melded with electric guitar, honky-tonk piano, harmonica, and drums. The notes swelled, full-throated, then ebbed again as the melody played on.

Lisa sighed, savoring Michael's nearness, his faint scent of cocoa-butter sunscreen mingled with fresh air and sunshine.

That afternoon they'd strolled nearly two miles down the beach, then spread out a blanket to picnic and bask in the sun. Lisa could almost still feel the blazing sand beneath her feet, hear the sharp cries of the seabirds swooping above them.

Where had the time gone? Being alone with Michael had been like a fleeting glimpse of paradise, ill-advised and foolish though it was.

She leaned closer into him, linking both arms around his neck. *"Galveston, oh Galveston. . . ."* Yes, Galveston. What beautiful memories. For as long as she lived, she'd never forget her day here with Michael.

Tomorrow she'd return to reality. Tomorrow she'd deal with the difficulties of her new life. But for now, she admittedly needed an escape.

She looked up at him. Their gazes caught and held. "Like to dance, Lisa?" he asked huskily, brushing her ear with his lips.

"Mmm — love to."

"Good, because I intend to dance your socks off." He chuckled. "Right till the stroke of midnight." He kissed the tip of her nose and smiled down at her. His deep blue eyes sparkled, teasing and caressing her all at the same time.

"Oh, yes!" She returned his banter. "The proverbial Cinderella story. Prince Charming whisks Cinderella away from the wicked stepmother — er, Dr. Woodstock in this case — and they live happily —" She bit off her words. *No, Lisa! There's no such thing as fairy tales and happy endings. At least not for you.*

She thought she detected a shadow flicker across his handsome face, but it was soon blotted out by his returning smile.

Ah, Lisa, he thought. *My sweet, disillusioned one. So small and pretty. If there were*

114

only some way I could get my hands on that jerk who broke your heart. Every time I think about him, I have all I can do to keep from wringing his arrogant neck.

"I wonder what happened to Claudette and Rita?" he asked, looking around. The song ended. "They asked us to meet them here before the dance started." He glanced at his watch and pursed his lips. "That was nearly an hour ago."

"Probably got sidelined by Danny, the drummer." She scanned the sidewalks that were teeming with people. There were no signs of Claudette and Rita anywhere. "I bet he introduced them to a couple of his buddies who'd tagged along," she added. And if that was the case, then hats off to Danny. Hopefully it would distract Rita from going after Michael.

"Well, help me keep an eye out for them, will you? Even though Claudette's perfectly capable of taking care of herself, I'm still her brother. Her *only* brother. Dad would expect that of me."

"Of course. Think we should walk down the street and start looking?" she asked. As much as she wanted to put off meeting the two women again, she couldn't help sharing Michael's concern.

"Yeah, maybe for just a block or two." A

small frown puckered his brow. "But it's still early. No point getting worried yet."

As they threaded their way through the crowd, they passed by an antique store, an art gallery, and a small antique and gift shop. The rosy glow of the setting sun reflected off the store windows. The cement beneath their feet still radiated with warmth.

"What do you suppose happened to them?" he asked tightly, pushing his sunglasses onto his forehead. "Claudette might have her faults, but big-time tardiness isn't one of them."

"You and my brother Ralph," she said, hoping to dilute his concern. She disliked seeing him worry unnecessarily, yet at the same time his sense of responsibility to family warmed her. Without a doubt, if this had been Estelle instead, he would have been equally solicitous.

They slowed their pace, then stopped at a crosswalk and waited for the stoplight to change. A dozen or so teenagers dressed in oversized T-shirts and neon-colored shorts laughed and shouted as they paused beside them.

"I thought you and Ralph were separated most of the time," Michael said. The light flashed WALK and they stepped off the curb.

116

"We were. Ralph and I were always apart. But that didn't stop him from keeping tabs on me, especially after we became teenagers. All those years we lived in different foster homes, even the times we were hundreds of miles apart, he must've phoned at least three times a week."

"I suppose your traveling with Jessell and Stern is driving your brother crazy," Michael commented, smiling wryly.

"Yes . . . and no. He's got his own family now, a terrific wife and two beautiful children, a boy and a girl." She blinked hard, forcing back her envy. She and Charles had talked about having children too . . . but now her dreams of a family would never be. "When I called Doc Largent at the airport, I asked him to ring up my brother for me too," she continued a bit shakily. "I probably should try to phone both of them again."

The band launched into another tune, this time a rendition of an old Willie Nelson classic, "On the Road Again."

"Aha!" Michael exclaimed with a chuckle, his mood now lighter. "They're playing our song, Lisa!" He draped an arm across her shoulder and winked.

"I don't think Willie had the circus in mind when he recorded that piece," she teased him back.

"Nope, I suppose not." He shrugged. "But what the heck? Country and western bands, carnivals and circuses . . . I suppose all traveling entertainers have something in common. Want to dance again?"

"Actually, I'd rather get something to drink. All this dancing's made me thirsty."

"Good idea!" He nodded toward a string of fast-food concessions. "Let's head over and see what looks good and frosty."

Minutes later, they purchased two bottles of locally bottled sarsaparilla and lingered a while, listening to the music that blared from three blocks away through the sound system. Rita had been right, Lisa decided. Cloudburst was probably one of the best bands in the entire state of Texas.

Off in the distance sprays of multicolored fireworks glittered against a cobalt blue sky. Everywhere about them, people laughed and shouted. The carnival ambience was captivating.

Refreshed, they turned back to the street dance.

Michael caught Lisa's arm and asked, "How about it? Ready to dance some more?"

"Oh, yes!"

He took her hand in his, leading her to the sectioned-off area next to the band.

As they swayed to the music, he hummed

softly in her ear. She felt his breath fanning her cheek, the warmth of his strong, muscular body so dangerously close.

Her pulse rate quickened.

"Yo, Michael!" A familiar voice shattered the mood. They stopped dancing and turned around.

Claudette gave a quick wave as she elbowed her way closer. Rita trailed from behind.

"Where've you been?" Michael called. "Do you realize, Claudette, you're almost an hour and three-quarters late?"

"What's the big deal, Michael?"

"What's the big deal?" he echoed, raising a brow. The rhythm of the band faded into his clipped response. "It's not like you, that's what's the big deal. I mean, terrible things happen to people every day. And if you remember correctly, you're usually the one getting after me about being late."

She tossed him an offended look. "Don't forget, it was you who pointed out in the first place that Rita and I didn't need an escort service."

"All right." Michael held up both hands in a gesture of reconciliation. "So I did. Sorry. I . . . I didn't mean to overrea—"

Rita interrupted him. "Michael, I'm absolutely dying to dance, and it's obvious

Danny can't oblige me now. Come on. Just one time."

"Yeah, Michael!" Claudette quickly agreed. "Since this is Rita's favorite band, it'd be a crying shame if she didn't get to dance."

An artery in Michael's neck throbbed. "Sorry, ladies. I'm going to dance with Lisa."

"Michael, how rude," Claudette admonished. "The least you can do is try to make Rita feel welcome. So far, you've barely given her the time of day!"

Lisa's gaze flicked from Claudette to Michael. Without warning an idea popped into her mind. She'd better act now — this was the chance she'd been waiting for! What a perfect opportunity to confront Claudette while Michael was safely out of earshot.

"It's all right, Michael," Lisa said. "Go ahead. I'll sit — er, stand — this one out."

"Sure you don't mind?" he asked.

"Uh . . . no."

Lisa's heart turned over as she watched Michael take Rita by the arm and lead her through the crowd and onto the street.

Please, Michael. Make it only one dance, she silently pleaded. She forced her attention back to Claudette. The invisible shield of tension separating them was growing more uncomfortable by the moment.

She inhaled a steadying breath. "Thanks for your *elegant* hand-me-downs," she said, angling Claudette a long, hard look. "You're a fine one to talk about giving people a proper welcome."

"Oh, come on, Lisa. Lighten up. Where's your sense of humor?"

"You call that funny?"

"Why not? Besides, you can consider that your initiation into Jessell and Stern — one, I might add, you failed miserably. Just like you've failed miserably at everything else you've attempted so far."

"You're wrong, Claudette. I've failed no one. Especially you."

Smiling sardonically, Claudette narrowed her eyes. "Once a townie, always a townie. Right, Lisa?"

Lisa choked back her anger. Claudette's insinuation stung like a slap across the face. "Listen, Claudette. I don't care what you call me, but there's something I want you to know. You can relax, as far as Michael's concerned. I'm not some love-starved groupie. I don't intend to lure him away from —"

She broke off abruptly. Something in her peripheral vision had caught her attention. She turned and realized it was the flutter of a white tissue — Rita's white tissue. Though she and Michael were still dancing,

Rita was dabbing at the corners of her eyes. Michael appeared to be trying to comfort her.

Rita sent Michael a tremulous smile, then nodded slowly in response to whatever he'd just said. He smiled back and squeezed her arm.

Lisa struggled against a new stab of jealousy. What was happening? Could Rita be making up a sob story to win Michael's affection?

Quickly pushing her suspicions aside, she turned her attention back to Claudette. "As I was saying —" She hesitated, looking around. "Claudette? Did you hear me? Are you still there?"

Michael's twin was nowhere in sight.

Michael swerved off the highway and parked the truck alongside a deserted stretch of beach. "Let's walk some more," he murmured, staring off into the darkness. "I'm not ready to go home yet."

"All right."

The entire way there, he'd been unusually quiet. Back at the Strand, only seconds after he and Rita had finished dancing, Claudette had cornered them. For several minutes — an eternity, to Lisa — they'd stood well away from the crowds talking among themselves, their expressions serious.

"Is something wrong, Michael?" she asked quietly as they strode down the beach. His hand was warm, wrapped around hers. "I mean, why was Rita crying back at the dance? And why the long talk with Claudette and Rita afterward?"

"It's nothing," he replied, tight-lipped. He stopped, faced her squarely, then added, "Rita's just a little homesick, that's all."

"Are you sure?"

"Yes."

Lisa had to wonder about that. After all, if Rita had traveled with a circus previously, then she should certainly be accustomed to being away from home. No, there must be more. But whatever it was, Michael obviously wasn't ready to confide in her.

"Look, Lisa." He brushed his thumb over her palm. In the distance, a foghorn blared. "I . . . I don't want anything to spoil the rest of our day together. Let's not talk about it anymore."

She hesitated, her voice reluctant. "Well . . . all right, I guess." Maybe it was wrong, expecting him to share everything, she reasoned. After all, she'd only known Michael for a short time, just barely a month.

He smiled down at her, though the hint of a frown marred his features. The late-night breeze carried the scent of creosote and salt water. The breeze picked up, teased her hair, and tossed a strand across her eye. Gently he brushed it back off her forehead, allowing his hand to remain there.

As they started out again, a full moon inched higher, casting its whitewash over the long span of beach. The moonlight illuminated the sea foam, gossamer and wispy, skittering across the sand where the sea met the shore.

They paused to slip out of their shoes. The sand, cool and pliant beneath their bare feet, cushioned their footfalls as they walked on and on.

At times they chased each other, laughing, teasing, then flinging themselves into each other's arms. Other times, they strolled in quiet contemplation, hand in hand, pausing to stare into each other's eyes, neither speaking.

And when he finally turned and pulled her close, kissing her with tenderness and passion, she knew there was no turning back. Although Michael could never be hers, the truth loomed painfully clear.

She'd entrusted him with her heart.

From Texas, the circus pushed farther east, trundling through Louisiana, Mississippi, Alabama, then Georgia. All the while, Lisa held on to the memory of that extraordinary day in Galveston with Michael. During the times she felt most downhearted, which were often, the memories sustained her, spurred her on. Oh, for that precious hour or two at the end of each day when they could finally meet again to tend to the horses.

Yet while her heart was spinning wild, wondrous dreams about Michael, her head continued to issue loud warnings. Oh, yes, she may have fallen in love with him, but her love wasn't cast in stone. Had she already forgotten about her troubled past with Charles? And now her ever-uncertain future with Jessell and Stern?

Though Dr. Woodstock had remained every bit as difficult to please, at least he hadn't fired her. Maybe he figured for the meantime, an incompetent assistant was better than none at all — for no sooner had they handled one emergency than another one would crop up.

One day in New Orleans, for instance, a black bear broke its claw, and it became badly infected. Later a show horse tripped and fell in the ring, fracturing a leg. Then a lion needed a tooth extraction and her gums packed. The monkeys, camels, and elephants had their share of problems as well.

Lisa soon learned that the camels were the most difficult of all animals to anesthetize. Because the camel's neck was rippled with several layers of fat, it was hard to insert the needle into exactly the right spot.

Under Dr. Woodstock's watchful eye, she found herself ever nervous and edgy. *He's gearing up for the evaluation,* she reminded herself. *It's already the middle of July. On D day, less than two weeks from now when my probation is up, he'll undoubtedly deliver the verdict.*

Her struggling efforts to help the trainers whenever their show animals needed medical care hadn't improved much either.

Oh, yes, there had been those minuscule victories, those times she'd managed to coax one of the huge creatures to cooperate, or offer an innovative approach to an old problem. For a short-lived moment, she'd felt as she imagined Michael must feel whenever he caught a difficult trick — a grandiose rush of satisfaction, a mountaintop experience. But all too quickly another near disaster would strike.

Unfortunately, the disasters far outnumbered the mountaintop experiences.

One evening after another exhausting day, Lisa trudged back to Estelle's trailer, her spirits at an all-time low. The weather was hot and humid, the temperatures hovering at nearly one hundred. Her T-shirt clung to her, moist and clammy.

Most of the time, in hot, humid climates, she wore cutoff jeans or shorts, cotton T-shirts, and sandals — just as she had today. Now she could hardly wait for a refreshing shower and the chance to change.

"Hi there, Lisa!" Michael's mother waved as she stepped outside the motor home. "Got a minute?" One of her show poodles, Rags's sister, was tucked into the crook of her arm.

"Hello, Mrs. Figaro!" Lisa waved back.

Off to one side, three young children rode tricycles, causing swirls of dust to rise up about them.

Mrs. Figaro was dark-haired, pretty, and petite, much like Estelle. She smiled warmly. "What's with this Mrs. Figaro business? I've already given you permission to call me Olivia."

"All right. Olivia it is."

"I'm fixing fried chicken tonight," Olivia went on, shading her eyes against the sun. "Would you like to stop by later tonight to join the girls and myself?" She hesitated, a smile tugging at the corner of her mouth. "Or are you and Michael going to fix something to eat at his place again?"

"I . . . I'm not sure yet. But fried chicken sounds wonderful. I'll try to make it." She smiled her appreciation.

Actually, she and Michael had only shared a meal at his trailer a few times before. Though Lisa was eager to get to know Michael's mother better, she didn't relish the possibility of having to face Claudette again — especially not after their confrontation back in Galveston.

Lisa unlocked Estelle's trailer and stepped inside. Rags greeted her, wagging his tail and nipping at her ankles.

"Hello, you poor thing," Lisa said as she ducked down to scratch the poodle under his chin. "How can you stand this heat on a day like today?"

The dog gave an excited bark as Lisa started rummaging through the small closet she and Estelle shared in search of her coolest tank top.

Unexpectedly she spotted Claudette's oversized green blouse on a heap at the bottom. It was finally time to take action. Either she'd have to throw it away or deliver it back to Claudette.

Remembering a large Dumpster behind the north wall of the auditorium, she decided to discard it there. She showered and dressed quickly, then placed the blouse in a brown shopping bag and crossed the lot toward the Dumpster.

The evening show was in full swing. She paused to linger by the open backdoor of the auditorium. Music drifted from inside. Hot dog vendors worked the side aisles, while men, women, and children stared in awe at the kaleidoscope of activity inside the three rings.

It'd been nearly two weeks since she'd attended a performance, she realized. She adored watching the Flying Figaros, especially Michael. And the opportunities had been far too seldom.

She took a front-row seat in the section reserved for the press and circus personnel, then settled back. In the center ring, Claudette was perched on top of a trapeze, balancing with both feet.

"Claudette's been working hard on her solo act," she remembered Michael telling her. Hopefully Lisa wasn't too late to see him too.

"Have the Flying Figaros already performed?" she asked a man with a red beard and laptop computer who sat next to her.

"Yes," he answered. "They finished about five minutes ago."

"Just my luck," Lisa muttered.

"What did you say?" He peered at her through Coke-bottle glasses.

"What I mean is," she amended, "I . . . I always seem to miss the best part."

"Maybe not. Watch this chick. She's sharp."

As Lisa looked on, she knew she had to agree. Dressed in a neon blue, sequin-studded leotard, Claudette looked stunning.

Yet Lisa sensed something was wrong. Claudette's stance appeared unsteady, her normal smile of confidence missing. In an instant, her knees buckled. Her arms started to flail. Then she tumbled downward. A gasp rose from the audience.

"Close call!" the guy next to her exclaimed, straining forward on the edge of his seat. "Good thing for that safety net!"

"Yes, thank goodness," Lisa agreed, heaving a sigh. A strange mixture of relief and pity swept over her. Poor Claudette. Lisa's dislike for her unexpectedly gave way to concern.

Ghostly pale, Claudette leaped down over the side of the net and clutched the front of her leotard. Yet her efforts failed to conceal the large rip that extended right down the middle.

Lisa's hand flew to her mouth in an effort

to suppress a giggle. So Claudette had ripped her costume and lost her focus. No wonder she'd fallen. . . .

Suddenly Lisa recognized her golden opportunity. Springing to her feet, she snatched the blouse from inside the bag and rushed into the ring. Then in one quick motion, she draped the blouse over Claudette. *Saved by the sickening green fabric,* Lisa silently cheered. Right back home where it belonged.

At that moment, she had to confess, she was more interested in adding to Claudette's embarrassment than covering up the rip. But the crowd was loving it! The sound of their applause rose. Louder and louder. In no time, they had risen to their feet and were waving their arms and cheering wildly.

Claudette flashed the audience her most dazzling smile as she dipped into a sweeping bow. For a split second her eyes met Lisa's.

As Lisa hurried back to the bleachers, she blinked hard. She couldn't believe what she'd just done.

Then the truth hit her like a meteorite crashing to earth. Claudette had changed her blunder into victory. She'd made it appear as if, all along, Lisa's entrance was part of the act.

It was the mark of a true entertainer, Lisa mused, shaking her head. Without a doubt, Claudette had what it took to turn things around.

But the big question remained, did Lisa have it too?

Chapter Eight

"Hoshi," Lisa called to the stable boy from the far side of the horses' tent, "I need to leave a little early tonight to talk with Dr. Woodstock. Will you please finish up here and see that the rest of the horses get fresh feed and water?"

"Sure, no problem." He looked up from the opposite side of the tent. Beneath a large spotlight, he stood brushing down a white Arabian. "Is something wrong, Lisa? Why do you have to talk with the doc?"

"Diamond might have a sinus infection. It's not an emergency, of course, but she might need antibiotics."

He nodded. "I noticed she's looked a little listless lately."

"Yes, and she's dragging her head — a sure sign." Diamond was one of the two black liberty horses that performed with Ebony.

Lisa squatted down and placed her hand between the animal's thighs, then added, "Hmm. I think she's also running a fever."

Though Lisa and the veterinarian

checked all the horses' temperatures routinely twice a day, she'd have to make certain from now on to monitor Diamond more often, she told herself. In hot Southeastern climates such as this, horses sweated off most of their water. A high fever might only hasten dehydration.

"Are sinus infections contagious?" Hoshi asked. "Do we need to worry about the other horses too?"

"It all depends. This condition usually starts from a virus, a common cold. But horses can be prone to the bacterial complications that sometimes affect their sinus passages."

Thank goodness, Ebony was staying hale and hearty, Lisa thought, as she wandered over to where the mare had been tied. She gave her a pat on the snout, then offered her a handful of oats in her opened palm.

Ebony snorted, eyed Lisa with velvety brown eyes, then munched down the feed.

"Good Ebony. Nice girl," Lisa crooned. "I'm afraid you and I won't get to ride tonight. But maybe tomorrow night, okay?"

Lisa's bonding with the horse was growing stronger with each passing day. She could well understand Edward Figaro's affection for Ebony. According to Estelle, he'd asked about her nearly every time Olivia had phoned him.

Lisa glanced at her watch. What was taking Michael so long? After tonight's show, his fans — especially the groupies — had pressed in like a swarm of bees attacking a honeycomb. Though Michael was always courteous, pausing to chat, sign his autograph, and answer questions, this time he was uncustomarily late.

What would he say about Claudette having fallen? Lisa wondered uneasily. And especially about the way she herself had intervened? Since Lisa had never told him about the nasty trick Claudette had played on her, he wouldn't understand the real meaning behind what Lisa had just done. Maybe he was angry with her. Maybe that's why he was staying away.

She emerged from the tent and looked first right, then left, in hopes of spotting him. Though dusk had settled over the circus grounds, she could see people milling about. Michael wasn't one of them. Farther down at the elephant kraal, a square of portable sheds, two keepers were hard at work oiling the massive creatures' dry, leathery hides with mops and buckets.

At last she spied him striding in her direction. His eyes were downcast. He appeared lost in thought.

135

"Michael!" she called to him and waved. "Over here!"

"I'm coming," he said, lifting his gaze. "Sorry I'm late. I got a little waylaid after the show talking with my sisters and —"

"Michael," Lisa interrupted him. "I think Diamond has a sinus infection. She's hanging her head and running a fever."

He ran a hand through his hair, sighed heavily, and hitched his thumbs in the back pockets of his jeans. "Maybe I've been working her a little too hard. Have you mentioned it to Doc?" he asked.

"Not yet. I'm going to in just a few minutes."

"Lisa —" His eyes bore into hers, his expression wary. Something told her he was no longer thinking about the show horses.

Her stomach dropped. "What is it, Michael?"

"We need to go somewhere to talk. Someplace where we can be alone."

"Michael, if you're upset about what I did tonight to Claudette, I swear I can explai—" She stopped abruptly. Dare she change her mind and tell him? Would he believe his sister could've been so contemptible?

"No, it's not that, Lisa. Right now, I've got other things to worry about."

She caught her breath. "What's wrong?"

She hadn't seen such a troubled look on his face since the night Ed had told them about his brother's passing.

"I . . . I'll explain in a minute. Let's head over to my trailer. Now."

She hesitated.

"But Diamond . . . Dr. Woodstock —"

"You can catch up with Doc later." His gut twisted so badly he felt like doubling over. If he didn't talk with Lisa now, he might lose his nerve. She'd never understand. Never in a million years. But then in all fairness, how could he expect her to?

"All right, Michael. Let's go." She felt her mouth grow dry, her muscles tense.

They started off, an arm's length between them. Two daredevil motorcyclists wearing shiny metallic riding suits passed by. Lisa noticed one of them make eye contact and send her a suggestive smile, but her awareness of him was fleeting and inconsequential. The unspoken tension between Michael and herself was becoming more charged with each passing moment.

At last they arrived at the trailer. He held the door open, waiting for her to enter first. Then he stepped in and flicked on a small table lamp. A dim glow illuminated the compact interior.

"Sit down," he said, gesturing to the

daybed against the opposite wall.

She did, glancing about. As before, the same thought struck her. Michael could benefit from a woman's decorative touch.

Though clean and tidy, his living quarters were Spartan, lacking the special details that characterized Estelle's. Apparently unfazed when Lisa had offered suggestions, he'd jokingly referred to it as his bachelor's retreat.

But tonight, she could tell he was in no mood for jokes.

As he eased down on a folding chair directly across from her, worry lines creased his forehead. Hunching forward, he stared down at the floor and clasped his hands tightly together.

"So what is it?" Lisa asked, scarcely taking a breath. She prayed that nothing had changed between them. But the edge in his voice only underscored her misgivings.

He looked up and met her gaze. "Tonight after the show, Uncle Rudy, my sisters, and I had a long talk. That's why I was late."

"A talk about what?"

"About where the troupe is headed. About our future with Jessell and Stern." He flicked his gaze away from her, then pulled it back, hesitating. "Actually, we first started talking about it back at the street dance in Galveston. When you asked me about it later that night on the beach, I didn't want to tell you because everything was so uncertain. But now that's changed. We know for sure what we must do."

"So . . ." she prompted.

"So we're adding a new member to the troupe. Rita."

Her heart lurched. "Rita?"

"Uh-huh. It's time we expand our act . . . and . . . in order to do that, we need a fourth flyer."

"Why?" she gasped. "Why would you need Rita?" Her thoughts skittered back to that day on the horse-drawn tram when Claudette had foreseen this. Was Michael planning to leave again?

He faltered, his eyes dark with . . . with what? Pain? Regret? *Deceit?*

"We just do," he answered. She could see his Adam's apple moving. "We need Rita."

"But . . . but, whose idea was it anyway?" Lisa asked. "Who decided you needed a fourth flyer?"

"Claudette did. I did. All of us, I guess."

"I see," she said, pressing her hands against her temples. Her head pounded. No, if Michael was leaving he would surely tell her so. The reason for the new flyer was his interest in Rita. Without a doubt, Claudette was responsible for this cozy arrangement.

But what had happened to Michael's resolve? In the beginning, at least, he'd been savvy to Claudette's intentions. He'd said that Claudette was determined he marry another aerialist. Couldn't he figure out what was happening now?

"But there's one major problem," he continued. "Though Rita's pretty good at flying, she's been away from it for a while. She's going to need tons of practice to catch on to our routines."

"Then why didn't you pick someone else?" Lisa asked, pointing out the obvious.

"There is no one else. At least no one else we could get on short notice. Rita is the logical choice." He rose, exhaled slowly, and turned away. Silently he stared out the small window next to the trailer door, propping his hands on his hips. The only sound was a ticking clock coming from somewhere in the back.

At last he turned around and sat next to her on the daybed, only inches away. He pinned her with his gaze. "In the beginning — when you first came to Jessell and Stern — I told you we wouldn't be seeing much of each other."

"And you were right," she agreed. "You and I both put in long, exhausting days."

"Yes, we do — though somehow we've

140

managed to eke out an hour or two together at the end of each day." A wry smile lifted one corner of his mouth as he added, "I guess that's only been possible because we've combined business with pleasure."

"But at least we managed," she said in a small voice. Was Michael suggesting that their time together had meant to him more business than pleasure? Had he only been using her to help him with the horses?

He reached for her hand, clasping it tightly. "Yes, we did manage," Michael agreed. "But I'm afraid, now . . . I'm afraid things will have to be different for a while."

"You don't want me to help you with the horses any longer?" she asked. "Or come here anymore after the work's done?" Was he giving her the brush-off? Did he plan to spend all his free time with Rita?

He met her gaze, but for a long moment refrained from answering. The lamplight illuminated his profile, the tight and uncustomary downturn of his mouth. His nearness was bittersweet.

"No," he said at last. "It's not that I don't want your help. In fact, it's just the opposite. You and Hoshi and the other stable boys may have to get along without me for a while. Now that we're breaking Rita in, I'll have to spend more time than ever practicing — especially each night after the last show."

"But what about your promise to your father, Michael? He's put his trust in you to look after the show horses, especially Ebony."

Michael's face darkened. "I haven't forgotten about that. But Pop will understand when he comes back and learns the circumstances. He'll have to."

Visions of Charles swam up in her mind. Hadn't it been the same with Charles and Ramona? Hadn't he insisted their last-minute meetings were only for professional reasons?

Lisa blinked twice, forcing the memory to the farthest corner of her mind. *Don't let it happen again. Michael's ruse is no different than Charles's. Take back your heart — before it's too late.*

"Lisa?" Michael's voice cut through her thoughts.

"Yes?"

"You understand, don't you?" He stroked back her hair and rested his hand on her neck.

His touch threatened to disarm her. She yearned to wrap her arms around him, beg him to change his mind about Rita — but knew she couldn't.

"Certainly," she lied, avoiding his eyes. After all, Michael had no claims on her, she reminded herself. He'd never even said he loved her. Unmistakably, his caresses, his kisses, had amounted to nothing more than overactive male hormones.

"Good." His thumb moved gently back and forth against her jaw. Instinctively she pulled away. "And one more thing. Don't say anything about this to the others yet, will you?"

"The other circus people?"

"Yes. Mom too. Especially Mom."

"Why? They'll see the four of you practicing. It'll be obvious."

"Maybe. Maybe not. Everyone's usually too busy to pay that much attention."

"But what's the big secret, Michael?"

"I can't say. Not yet anyway. I've made a promise to Claudette. I gave my word to keep quiet."

"Can't you get out of it? The way you got out of your promise to her that day you met me at the airport?"

"I'm afraid not." He set his jaw. His face remained unreadable. "This promise is different."

Jessell and Stern continued to press on. To Lisa's relief, Diamond's sinus infection had been easily cured. After a big dose of antibiotics and a little extra tender, loving care, the liberty horse was soon back in center ring.

Once again, Michael was right. Their time together was becoming increasingly rare. What was more, she sensed his growing preoccupation with whatever was bothering him. The few moments they did have together, he seemed troubled. Distracted. Even Estelle was ill at ease lately.

Lisa speculated that perhaps Estelle was struggling to shake off her own disappointment about Michael's sudden interest in Rita. That morning when Estelle had asked Lisa about her relationship with Michael, she'd been quick to give her stamp of approval.

Maybe too, Estelle was worried that Lisa would press her for details about what was going on. Yet, tempting as it was, Lisa promised herself she wouldn't do that. No, she wouldn't betray her friendship with Estelle by using her that way. Whatever it was, Lisa would have to discover it for herself.

Every moment possible, she lingered by the backstage door, especially late at night, to watch the Flying Figaros hard at practice. But each time she did, the hurt only burrowed deeper.

The troupe looked fabulous. Michael and Rita worked together in perfect harmony, almost as if they were made for each other. Maybe it was because he was not only a professional but also a gifted teacher. He seemed to know exactly what kind of help Rita needed and was the best one who could show her.

"When will Rita be ready to perform at the shows?" Lisa asked Michael every chance she could get. She hoped that once Rita's skills were up to par, perhaps they wouldn't need to practice so much.

But Michael's answer was always the same. "I can't say yet, Lisa. We need a little more time. The future's still too uncertain."

What future? she couldn't help thinking bitterly. The troupe's future? Or more to the point, Michael's future with Rita?

One night in Columbus, Ohio, while Jessell and Stern was packing for their next move and Michael and the troupe were busy at practice, Lisa started for the horses' tent to saddle up Ebony.

The mare was long overdue for a good run, Lisa decided, and truth was, Lisa needed some diversion too. Only three days • remained till her evaluation. Her stomach was a tangle of nerves.

Yes, Lisa needed time again with Ebony.

145

She would never tire of galloping into the night, the wind smarting her face, the clopping of Ebony's hoofbeat, rhythmic and reassuring, beneath her. Now the anticipation buoyed her, helped compensate for the reality that she could no longer share this time with Michael.

Inside the shadowy tent, she squinted for a moment, allowing her eyes to adjust to the portable overhead light. The stable boys had brought in fresh hay, feed, and water. The place looked clean, with everything in order. Good thing they were doing such a great job, Lisa thought. Michael hadn't set foot here for over a week — at least not as far as she knew.

Immediately she heard a sound, a horse grunting. She strained her ears to hear better. It seemed to be coming from the farthermost corner where Ebony was tied.

She edged closer, then gasped at the sight that greeted her. Ebony lay on the ground rolling from side to side. Her face was tense. Her breathing was rapid and shallow. Seeing Lisa, the horse made a feeble attempt to heave to her feet, then crumpled back down again. She let out another grunt and rolled over.

Every nerve in Lisa's body seemed to stand at alert. *Colic!* She and Doc Largent had treated a stallion with colic only weeks before Lisa had left Long Island. The horse had nearly died. Ebony showed all the classic symptoms.

"Don't you dare keep rolling!" Lisa cried, fighting back panic. She had to stop Ebony. Rolling could cause her intestines to twist, shutting off the blood supply and eventually poisoning her. And if her intestines were already twisted, then rolling would only make it worse.

Hands trembling, Lisa fastened the halter and coaxed Ebony into a standing position. No one else was around to help. Not any of the stable boys. Not Hoshi.

With measured gait, she began walking the horse out from the tent and into the lot.

Lisa's mind raced. She needed to find Dr. Woodstock! She needed to find him fast! How long had Ebony been ill? Why hadn't anyone else found her?

But on second thought, she couldn't lay blame on the stable boys. It was Michael who was at fault. He'd made a promise to Ed Figaro. Ebony was Michael's responsibility. Clearly Michael had let his father down.

Lisa tugged at the horse's halter and quickened her pace, but Ebony stopped in her tracks and refused to go on. Her eyes were glazed over with pain. The sweat beaded on her hide, glistening beneath the glare of a streetlight. Then the mare flopped down again and started to thrash.

"Come on, girl," Lisa pleaded. "Get up! Stay on your feet." Lisa caught sight of Walter as he jumped down from inside one of the semitrailers that hauled the elephants.

"Walter!" she hollered. "Come here! Quick!" He rushed to meet her, then dropped his gaze to Ebony. "Oh, no!"

"Yes." Lisa puffed. "Colic, I suspect. Help me get Ebony up. We have to keep her walking." Together they urged the mare to her feet. "Have you seen Dr. Woodstock?" Lisa asked desperately.

"I talked with him about an hour ago. He and a few of the animal keepers were going to Hoshi's trailer. Today is Hoshi's birthday, and they're celebrating."

She thrust the halter into Walter's hand. "I need your help. Please don't let Ebony go down again! After I find Dr. Woodstock, I'll be right back!"

"You got it."

Lisa dashed off. The toe of her sneaker caught on a snag, and she nearly tripped. Righting herself, she kept running. In no time she arrived at Hoshi's trailer. The sounds of talking and laughter drifted from inside.

Someone was standing in the open doorway. Peering inside, Lisa realized to her relief that it was the vet.

"Dr. Woodstock!" she called. "Please! Come quickly!"

"What's the matter?" he asked, his voice fringed with irritation.

"It's Ebony! S-she's in a lot of pain! Sweating. Thrashing about. Colic . . . I think." Lisa stopped to try to catch her breath.

"What?" His mouth dropped open. "Colic, you say?"

"Yes . . . at least I suspect so. I found her alone about a half an hour ago . . . rolling. The stable boys . . . they were nowhere in sight. So I started walking her, then I found Walter. He's trying to keep her on her feet right now!"

Instantly the irritation melted from his face. "I'll take a look at her, Lisa! Right away."

"Yes, hurry!" As they broke into a fast stride, it suddenly dawned on her. For the first time, Dr. Woodstock had addressed her by her first name.

"The reason you couldn't find any of the stable boys was because most of them were with Hoshi," the vet explained, three paces ahead of her. "It's a good thing Walter knew my whereabouts." The admiration in his voice was unmistakable. "Good work, Lisa. If a colicky horse isn't kept walking, the consequences could prove fatal."

At the thought, Lisa shuddered. "I know that." A swell of pride momentarily nudged away her fear for Ebony. Dr. Woodstock's praise was sincere, she could tell. He was no longer treating her like an outsider.

"We'll start treatment right away," he was saying. "First try to rule out any of the more serious possible causes."

"Like a twisted intestine?" she asked.

"That's right." He pursed his lips, then frowned.

"First we must give Ebony a shot into her neck vein to bring down any inflammation. If the intestine is indeed twisted, the medication might relax it sufficiently so it'll correct itself. I may need to do a rectal exam too and see if I can feel anything."

They found Walter walking Ebony at the spot where Lisa had left them. Immediately all three got to work. But after Dr. Woodstock had administered the injection and Ebony's condition hadn't improved, Lisa's hopes paled.

The vet snapped off his rubber gloves and shook his head. "Yep. Just as I feared. We don't dare wait any longer. I'll call ahead to the nearest equine surgical center. Walter, go fetch the stable boys. Have them line up a driver. Lisa, you stay here with Ebony."

Fresh fear gripped her. "She's going to need an operation?"

"Yes. The sooner, the better."

His confirmation hit Lisa like a death knell. In only minutes, Ebony would be loaded into a horse trailer and shipped off. Dear, beautiful, wonderful Ebony.

"May I go with her?" she pleaded. "Someone's going to have to keep her up till they get to the surgical center."

"No, you'd better stay. I might need your help in the event another emergency arises. Hoshi can ride along instead."

"Okay." She couldn't stop her hands from trembling. What if she never saw the mare again?

Lisa stood next to Dr. Woodstock watching the truck and horse trailer cart Ebony down the highway. The red taillights grew dim, smaller, then faded into the darkness.

Tears swam before her eyes.

"Are you all right, my dear?" he asked. "Would you like me to stay with you for a while?"

Backhanding a tear that had escaped down her cheek, she sent him a tremulous smile. "Thanks. I'll be fine. I . . . I just need to be alone for a while. I'll be good as new after I get some sleep."

"If you change your mind, let me know. I'll probably be up late doing paperwork anyway." All traces of gruffness had disappeared from his voice.

"Yes. Thanks again. Good night, Dr. Woodstock."

"Sleep well, Lisa."

She turned slowly on her heel, then started for the tight cluster of RVs. As she walked along, her gaze swept the deserted grounds. All was quiet except for an occasional screech of a monkey, the sound of an elephant trumpeting. Trunks, equipment, and props lay stored in trucks and trailers, waiting for the next morning's departure.

Without Ebony.

Ebony, Lisa silently pleaded, *please come back. Please don't die.* She licked at another salty tear, suddenly aware she was covered with gooseflesh.

The sound of approaching footsteps stopped her. She looked up.

"Michael!" Indignation flared. He'd missed it all! Throughout the entire crisis, he'd been nowhere around.

"I heard they took Ebony." His voice was

filled with fear and regret. "I heard it's serious."

"You bet it's serious!" she said hotly. "So serious Ebony might die." Her throat ached. She swallowed against the knot in her throat. "I . . . I found her alone . . . alone and thrashing on the ground. Ebony's got colic, the worst kind. . . ."

He let out a low groan. "Oh, no. Pop lost another show horse to colic. About this time last year."

"It's all your fault, Michael! If you'd been taking care of Ebony like you promised your father, this would've never happened."

"Wait a minute!" His jaw dropped. "You're blaming me for what happened to Ebony?" He reached down to grasp her shoulders, but she jerked back.

"Who else?"

"Look, Lisa! Even if I had checked on Ebony earlier tonight, I can't be there every minute with her. Maybe she would've gotten sick after I left. Maybe —"

"That's not the point. The point is you shirked your responsibility."

His eyes sparked with anger. "Don't be so darn smug. You just happened to walk in on Ebony at exactly the right time. That's all."

She had to look away. "Admit it, Michael.

Lately you've been so wrapped up in practicing, wrapped up in Rita, Ebony's been the last thing on your mind."

Lisa blinked, amazed at the spite she heard in her voice. Yet she couldn't help it. The anger, the jealousy . . . it'd been building for too long.

"You promised your father you wouldn't let anything happen to Ebony," she continued. "But now it has. All because of you and Rita. How are you going to explain when your father finds out?"

"Let's leave Rita out of this. And stop getting hysterical. Ebony's different. She's not going to die."

Lisa felt like throttling him. Why couldn't he come to grips with reality? His denial — not only of his responsibility towards Ed Figaro's best show horse, but now the possible consequences of her illness — was infuriating.

"Fine, then," she said bluntly. "Whatever you say, Michael. I won't bring up Rita again. Good night." Wheeling around, she stalked off.

"Lisa, wait! Don't leave!" He sprinted after her, but she kept walking. "Let's talk. I'm sorry. I didn't mean what I said about your getting hysterical, I was just trying to —"

"Don't follow me!" she tossed back, cutting him off.

"But why? Can't we at least talk?"

"I'm through talking to you, Michael! Your apologies won't mean squat when Ebony's dead and gone!"

Chapter Nine

"Dr. Woodstock! Are you there?" Lisa stepped inside the veterinarian clinic the following morning and looked around. Jessell and Stern had finished setting up on the sprawling county fairgrounds outside a small town in Indiana.

"Hello, Lisa." He smiled, lifted his lab coat off the hook on the door, and shrugged into it. "There's a fresh pot of coffee on. Help yourself."

"Thanks. I will." She poured a cup of the strong hot brew and sipped gratefully. Exhausted, she could hardly think straight. The remainder of the night, she'd slept fitfully, tossing and turning — thinking about Ebony, thinking about Michael.

All night long, her quarrel with Michael had played through her mind. She'd lashed out in frustration and fear, she knew. This wasn't the first time she'd regretted her impulsive behavior. Yet Michael was responsible for part of the blame, she quickly reminded herself. Some of her accusations had been true.

"Have you heard anything about Ebony?" she asked the veterinarian. She looked up at him over the brim of her coffee mug and searched his face.

"Yes. I phoned the surgical center a little while ago."

Lisa sucked in a deep breath. "And?"

"And the news is good." He smiled as he picked up a blue ceramic mug from the counter and filled it with coffee. "Incredibly good."

"Oh, thank goodness!"

"Yes, I couldn't agree more. I talked with the vet who performed the surgery, a Dr. Fairfield, I believe. She said the intestine was badly contorted, but Ebony pulled through better than expected. If she continues to recover without complications, we can send a driver to pick her up in about a week or so."

Lisa didn't know whether to laugh or cry. "Gosh, Dr. Woodstock! You'll never know how worried I've been."

He patted her shoulder, his smile growing wider. "Don't be too sure about that, my dear. Your worry showed."

"I'll get the word out to the stable boys and keepers right away," she volunteered. "I'm sure everyone else will want to know." She paused as a new thought intruded.

"What about the Figaros? Have they heard yet?"

"Michael has, but I'm not sure about the rest of the family. He stopped by to ask about Ebony nearly an hour ago."

"Was he upset?"

"Terribly. He appeared nearly beside himself . . . that is, till I could calm him down long enough to pass on the good news."

Served him right, she thought. But even if Michael's remorse had been sincere, surely he'd already absolved himself, put the horse completely out of his mind, and hurried back to Rita.

Last night while she lay awake she'd determined exactly what she must do. If Ebony did survive, Lisa would stay long enough to be assured of her successful recovery, then turn in her resignation. Day after tomorrow, her probation was up anyway.

Most likely she'd have to work two jobs to pull herself out of debt, but somehow she'd find a way. She'd struggle through whatever sacrifices were necessary to cloister herself from more heartache. Fat chance Michael would try to come after her — regardless of what Claudette had thought in the beginning.

"Lisa, before we get to work, may I have a word with you?" Dr. Woodstock's voice broke though her troubled thoughts.

"Uh . . . sure."

He pulled out a ladder-back chair from behind his desk. It screeched against the tiled floor. "Please make yourself comfortable."

She sat down hesitantly. From behind the desk, a radio played.

The vet paused to turn the volume down, then hitched himself onto a stool across from her. "I know I've been kind of tough on you lately, but as I'm sure you've discovered, this work is not for the fainthearted."

"Yes, I certainly have." She lifted one shoulder. "But I wasn't totally blind, Dr. Woodstock. Even in the beginning, I never expected a bed of roses. I was just a little naive as to exactly how hard it would be." A woman's lilting voice on the radio was announcing the weather forecast.

"Good." He clasped his hands behind his head and pursed his lips. "Then at least you didn't come here with any false expectations. Perhaps you already know that the other two assistants I hired this past year didn't work out. They both left voluntarily."

"Uh-huh, I heard."

"They were young, lacking experience

with zoo and circus animals — just like you," he continued. He studied her for a long, contemplative moment, then readjusted his dark-framed glasses. "And as far as I'm concerned, there's no point waiting any longer to talk about *your* work here."

Her heart sank. Though Dr. Woodstock hadn't a clue about her decision yet, she had hoped to leave in his good graces.

"All right, then." She lifted her chin. "I'll check into flight arrangements as soon as I can."

"No, no! I didn't mean that."

"Oh?"

"Of course not!" His face melted into a kind squint. "Last night, you removed any doubt I may have had about you." He fixed her with an apologetic look. "If it hadn't been for your quick action, getting Ebony back onto her feet and walking her, she would've surely died. You're doing an outstanding job, Lisa. I want you to stay. Without question."

"You do?" Her voice squeaked. The radio played on, this time an old Elvis tune.

"Yes. And . . . and I'm sorry if I made life hard for you these past several weeks. I don't mean to come on so gruff, but sometimes I'm afraid I do."

"You're exhausted, just like me," she said,

her voice fringed with new understanding.

"Perhaps. But I won't attempt to make excuses for myself. I guess the reason the other assistants left was partly my fault too. Despite what they say about not teaching old dogs new tricks, I do intend to change. I promise you things will improve. You and me . . . we're going to make a terrific team, Lisa. I really mean that."

She let out a long, weary sigh. "Oh, Dr. Woodstock. Thank you for the vote of confidence. Your encouragement means a lot to me. But — but. . . ." She faltered, uncertain how to go on. At last she informed him about her decision to resign.

"I guess I'm not cut out for a life of continuous travel after all," she added, sidestepping the real issue. "I'm worn out, and maybe a little homesick also. Michael told me that someday all the towns and freeways would start to look the same." She let her breath out slowly. "Well, I guess he was right."

"Are you sure, my dear?" His dark brown eyes mirrored his disappointment. "Are you sure I'm not the reason?"

"I'm positive."

He cleared his throat. "Won't you give it a little while longer till you make your final decision? I realize it's been quite an adjustment — it was for me when I first came here five years ago too — but I guarantee it, the worst is over."

The disc jockey was about to announce the next song. In minutes the familiar title drifted into the clinic. *"Galveston, Oh Galveston . . ."*

Suddenly she felt the Texas heat warming her face, heard the waves crashing onto the beach, and saw Michael's face smiling down at her as they ran barefoot through the moist, cool sand.

A swirl of emotion washed over her. She would hold on to the memory forever, tuck it safely away in a secret corner of her heart. And at some point in time, during that long, lonely future that stretched bleakly ahead, she would take it out again. She'd dust it off, remember, and smile through her tears. But not even memories could change the bitter truth. Michael would never be hers. Not as long as she lived.

"Lisa?" Dr. Woodstock's voice was gentle, nudging her back.

She got to her feet and rested her hand on the countertop to steady herself. "I'm sorry, Dr. Woodstock, but I've made up my mind. I know now there can be no turning back."

"Hey, babe! Where're you headed?"

162

Lisa hesitated, then slowed her pace. Who was that? she wondered impatiently. It was the end of another long day. She was heartbroken and weary. All she wanted to do was phone her brother, tell him about her plans to leave, and turn in for the night. For two whole days now, she and Michael hadn't exchanged one word.

"I said, where're you headed?" The voice grew more insistent.

She turned around and recognized the good-looking stunt motorcyclist, the one who'd sized her up that night she and Michael were walking to his trailer.

"Come here. Talk to me. What's going on?" He jerked his head to one side, sending her a self-assured smile.

She smiled back at him, suddenly flattered. "I . . . I was just headed over to the phone booth at the front of the arena." Her smile grew wider as she thought. Why not give Michael a taste of his own medicine? Why not show him? Far be it from her to sit around all teary-eyed, pining after the likes of the superstar himself.

The guy sauntered up to her, giving her the once-over. "Like some company tonight?"

"Well . . . sure. But I . . . I don't believe we've met. At least not officially." He was even better looking up close — a trifle taller than Michael perhaps, only his hair was close-cropped, a shade darker with a tawny cast. Tonight he wore tight-fitting jeans and a white T-shirt with the Jessell and Stern logo.

He chuckled, crossing his muscular arms across his thick chest, causing the shirt to strain. "No, I guess we haven't met. But believe me, Lisa Prentice, I've been keeping close tabs on you."

"Oh, have you?" she asked coyly, flashing him her most stunning smile. "So what's your name?"

"Patrick. Patrick O'Brien."

"Hmm, an Irishman, no less."

"Uh-huh. Second generation." His green eyes laughed down at her with a teasing awareness. "So you like Irishmen, eh?"

"Well . . ." She stalled with her answer in an effort to flirt back.

"Not even a wee bit?"

"I adore Irishmen."

"Good. At least we've got that much straight. But tell me. Can your phone call wait?"

"Yes, I suppose so," she answered cautiously. What was he leading up to?

"I hope you're not planning on tying up with Figaro tonight," he said matter-of-factly.

"No. Why?"

"I just saw him and that new showgirl pretending they were hard at work. The rest of the flyers were nowhere in sight."

She set her jaw, struggling to hold her suspicions at bay. Were Michael and Rita doing more than just practice? Or was Patrick lying in hopes of furthering his own agenda? With difficulty she shrugged it off and met Patrick's smile again.

He sidled up to her a little closer. "Wanna go for a ride? On my bike?"

She remembered the way during performances he'd zoomed through the air over a low string of barrels. If he meant that, he was out of his head. "Y-your motorcycle?" she stammered.

"No, my dirt bike. I've got two, one for each of us. How 'bout you and me kickin' up a little dust in that big field behind the back lot?"

"Well . . ." She stalled some more. "I've never driven anything other than a car before — and a hot cycle when I was a little kid. But I have carved down some pretty wild slopes when I was into snowboarding," she added, not wanting to sound like a complete coward. No point telling him about the accident though.

"No sweat. You can sit nice and snug behind me and let me do the driving." He cocked his head to one side. "Besides, it's early. Nobody around here turns in before midnight. After we're done riding, maybe we can head out for some music. I know of a cool little club down the road."

"All right. Let's go."

On their way back to Patrick's truck and trailer where he stored his bikes, they came up behind Estelle, Claudette, and Olivia, who were sauntering along, absorbed in conversation. As far as Lisa could tell, they had no inkling that she and Patrick were behind them. It felt strange, though, to be with Patrick instead of Michael.

"Killer workout . . . Michael's almost got Rita flying triples. . . ." At first Lisa could only catch snatches of the conversation between the two sisters, who were positioned on either side of their mother.

So Patrick was right, Lisa realized with a sinking feeling. Michael had ended the practice early in order for Rita and him to work out alone. Deep inside, she had hoped Patrick was lying.

"I don't like this one bit." Olivia Figaro's voice, louder now, pulled Lisa from her thoughts. The woman's shoulders were slumped as the three quickened their pace. "Michael's working himself to a frazzle," she continued. "My son's exhausted and pale. Are you kids sure a fourth flyer is really necessary? Does Michael need to spend so much time coaching Rita?"

"Yes, Mom," Claudette answered levelly, her voice empty of all feeling. "We're sure."

"Sis," Estelle said, sending Claudette a furtive look. "Don't you think it's time —" She tossed a glance over her shoulder, then bit off her words.

The color drained from her face when she caught sight of Patrick and Lisa striding behind them.

In the moonlit lot next to the fairgrounds, Lisa sat close behind Patrick on his dirt bike, roaring across the rolling terrain. Full tilt, they mounted the next crest, then dipped again, spewing forth a trail of dust behind them.

What an absolute thrill, Lisa thought as the shadowy landscape whizzed by. The whine of the engine, the rush of adrenaline, the heady sensation of freedom and speed! The only thing that would make it better would be if Michael could see her right now . . . which might not be too unlikely if Estelle had decided to tell him.

They rode on and on. Patrick gunned the engine as he cut a wide swath in the dirt, then came noisily to a stop.

Laughing, Lisa tossed back her head and adjusted her helmet. "Oh, please! Just one more time, Patrick! Please don't stop now!"

He angled a look over his shoulder, grinning broadly. "Like that, babe?"

"I loved it!"

"All right! Here we go again. Hold on tight!"

"Lisa Prentice!" Michael shouted from the edge of the field. Lisa struggled to hold back a smile. It was working . . . just as she'd hoped. Michael's voice grew louder as he strode directly toward them. "What are you trying to do, Lisa? Kill yourself?"

"What's the matter?" she asked. "Patrick's a pro. He's not going to let us crash."

"He's a daredevil biker!" Michael insisted, tight-lipped.

"Hey, man. Lay off. You heard the little lady!" Patrick glowered as he swung his leg over the side of the bike and got to his feet.

"*You* lay off, O'Brien!" Michael shot back.

"Get out of here, Figaro. Lisa's mine tonight!" He planted his feet wide, his stance unmistakably defensive.

"Michael! Patrick! Stop this minute!" Lisa broke in desperately, just as Patrick took a swing at Michael but missed by a narrow margin. She'd just wanted to stir up a little jealousy in Michael — not have them punch each other out.

"Please! Both of you!" she hollered, her voice rising. "Stop right now."

"Lisa, come on," Michael ground out, righting himself as he tugged at her hand.

"But Patrick and I aren't done yet! We're still —"

"Yeah, get out of her face, Figaro!" Patrick interrupted. "Who invited you here in the first place?"

"Lisa. Please." Michael's voice was steeped with forced control. "Let's go. *Now.*"

A pang shot through her. She longed to do as he asked, but her pride held fast. Hesitantly she met his gaze. His eyes were steady, uncompromising. She knew in an instant she could resist him no longer.

"You win, Michael," she said in barely a whisper, yanking off her helmet and handing it to Patrick. She turned back to him a second time, but already Michael was hurrying her away. "Patrick, I'm sorry, but thanks anyway. It was fun."

"Sure, babe. Come look me up when you change your mind," he hollered after them, his voice fringed with sarcasm.

By the time they'd reached his trailer, Michael was still gripping her hand so tightly, he'd caused it nearly to go numb. "Lisa, what in the heck's come over you, going off with O'Brien like that? As soon as Rita and I were done rehearsing, Estelle found me. She told me she'd seen you with him."

She squirmed beneath his angry gaze. "What are you worried about, Michael? Riding on Patrick's dirt bike was perfectly safe. It was even his idea I wear a helmet, just like he was."

She couldn't help wondering about the motivation fueling Michael's anger. Jealousy as she'd hoped? Or had she simply assaulted his male ego?

"Helmet or no helmet, O'Brien's still a daredevil stuntman," Michael said hotly. "And a pretty sleazy one at that."

"What are you talking about?"

"Haven't you heard? He was fired today. He's been ordered out of here first thing tomorrow."

"Why?"

"Unethical conduct. Pilfering. A whole list of stuff. Management has been keeping an eye on him for a long time. Finally they got enough evidence on him."

She gave an indifferent shrug, though her insides were churning. What if she *had* gone off later that night with Patrick?

170

"So you rescued me, Michael," she said. "I assure you, though, I'm perfectly capable of taking care of myself."

"Maybe you are. But meanwhile, I need to talk to you." He dug inside his hip pocket and produced the key to his truck.

"Whatever it is, make it fast. I'm tired."

"You weren't too tired to hang out with O'Brien," he reminded her, the edge in his voice still apparent.

"That's beside the point." Truth was, she didn't trust herself to be alone with Michael. One certain smile, only a fleeting touch . . . that was all it would take for her to melt back into his arms.

"Let's go for a drive," he said impatiently, jangling the keys. He glanced over his shoulder as two clowns, still clad in baggy polka-dot costumes, ambled by.

"Can't we talk right here?"

"No."

Michael didn't drive far, but rather turned off the main highway onto a side road and brought the truck to a stop beneath a grove of maple trees that hugged a meandering stream.

Rolling down his window, he released a slow, ragged breath. "I'm sorry," he began. "I'm sorry if I embarrassed you in front of O'Brien. But there's something else too. We

171

need to talk about what happened with Ebony."

She fixed her gaze on some indiscernible spot straight ahead. "We already did."

"I know. But I don't think you believed me the first time when I apologized. And . . . and I guess I can't blame you. I mean, just saying you're sorry must sound pretty lame after she nearly died."

"Yes. You're darned right it sounds lame." She swallowed hard. "But now since we've been told she's going to pull through, you don't have to beat yourself up anymore."

"Maybe. Maybe not."

Streams of moonlight slanted inside the truck, pearly and translucent. Crickets chirped, mingling with the soft sounds of the moving water. How she longed to feel the magic of his embrace. Feel his lips on hers. Hear him whisper how much he loved her. But here they were, their nerve endings raw and exposed, barely able to look at each other.

"I know how much you love Ebony," he continued. "We all do. I should've been watching her more closely. It was wrong to have left that up to you. After all, you're only one person too. You can't be with her all the time any more than I can."

"Have you told your father about what

happened?" she asked.

"I talked to Pop late last night after Mom phoned him for their weekly chat." He pinned her with a meaningful look. "And I gave you all the credit, Lisa. Every bit of it."

"Well, you *should* have."

"Pop was devastated, of course," he went on, ignoring her last remark. "He wanted to fly home on the spot, but I assured him that wouldn't be necessary." Michael reached out to take her hand, but she pulled it away.

"Now it's my turn to talk," she said, mustering up the courage she wasn't feeling inside. "There's something you need to know too, Michael, and I might as well get it over with right here and now."

"What?" He arched an eyebrow.

"As soon as Ebony comes back and I can see her again, I'm flying home."

"But why?"

"Why not?"

"Because Doc Woodstock wants you to stay. He's even told me so." Michael's voice broke as he avoided her eyes. "And so do I, Lisa."

"No, I must go. You were right from the start, Michael. I can never make a life for myself with Jessel and Stern. I should never have accepted Dr. Woodstock's offer in the first place. Next to getting involved with

Charles, it was the worst mistake I've ever made."

"But that's not true! *I* was wrong. So was everyone else who might've doubted you. You've already proven that when you saved Ebony. Don't go, Lisa. I want you to stay." He scowled. "Besides, it's high time you forget Charles."

"How can you say that? How can you say that while you keep shutting me away?"

"Shut you away?"

"Yes. We never see each other anymore. All you ever do is practice, practice, practice. And when I asked you about your promise to Claudette, you simply refused to answer me."

"It's not just me. Claudette's made us all swear not to tell. Estelle and Uncle Rudy too." The shadows from a swaying tree branch played across his face. "Just hang in there a little while longer. Will you, Lisa?"

"What for?" she asked. "It's obvious you'd rather be with Rita more than me. Your practices are simply a convenient excuse."

"You're wrong!"

She shook her head in disbelief. Her face grew warm as the blood pounded in her ears. "I saw the way you were trying to comfort Rita that night at the street dance, the way she was hanging on to you as if you were

174

the last male on earth. I might be on the outside track, Michael, but I'm not blind."

"You don't understand." He spread his hands wide and sighed again. "Rita was scared. Running scared. Like I told you before, our plans to bring Rita into the troupe all started that night in Galveston."

"If Rita's so scared, then I don't understand why you're forcing her!"

"I'm not. No one is. Rita wants this as much as anyone else. She just needs a lot of encouragement right now. And for the sake of the entire troupe, it's up to me to see she gets it."

He moved closer. He traced a finger down her cheek, never once taking his eyes off her.

"Michael, if you're so blasted concerned about Rita's confidence —"

"Shh! You've said enough."

His mouth crushed down on hers, putting an abrupt end to their conversation. His kiss was intense, hungry, and searching.

Torn with desire, she wrapped her arms around his neck and kissed him back — at the same time silently chastising herself. Why had she let down her guard? Why was she responding to him this way? Especially when she knew he was lying, filling her head with mere half-truths. Just like Charles. . . .

Heart pounding, she broke the contact.

"It's time to go, Michael. Please take me back."

"All right. Have it your way."

With a scowl, he turned the key in the ignition, then careened back onto the road.

Chapter Ten

Four days later — exactly one week after Ebony had been shipped off to the surgical center — the veterinarians there determined she could be returned to Jessell and Stern. Meanwhile, the circus was set up near a city west of Chicago in an empty lot adjoining a neighborhood shopping mall.

As Lisa and Dr. Woodstock waited inside the stabling quarters for Ebony's return, Lisa's stomach knotted with anticipation. Hoshi and the other stable boy who'd driven back to retrieve the mare were due to arrive soon.

The time without Ebony had seemed an eternity. Every day, Lisa had questioned Doc Woodstock for further progress reports, praying the horse hadn't suffered any complications. When the good news of Ebony's anticipated release finally arrived, she'd been overjoyed beyond words.

"How soon will it be before Ebony can go back in the ring?" Lisa questioned the veterinarian now as she hosed fresh water into the wooden trough. Ebony's stall had also been cleaned fastidiously. The sweet smells of fresh hay wafted about them.

"I'm not sure yet, Lisa," he answered from the opposite stall where he was checking another horse's temperature. "We'll have to see about Ebony's degree of strength and endurance. It shouldn't take too long though."

"I certainly hope not," Lisa said. Her mind wandered back to Ed Figaro and the Circus Hall of Fame. "The last thing Ed needs is to come back and find his best show horse unable to perform."

Only that morning, Estelle had informed her Ed had finally finished his business in Australia and would be returning home soon. At the thought, Lisa bit her lip. She would miss seeing him again. Back in the beginning before he was suddenly called away, while many of the circus folks had regarded her an outsider, he'd treated her with kindness and respect.

Yes, she would miss Michael's father greatly. But she'd already made her flight reservations, and postponing them would only make her parting more difficult. Tomorrow marked the fateful day. O'Hare International Airport, Chicago. Eleven A.M. She would leave the circus — and Michael — forever.

The sound of a truck motor, the crunch of tires against gravel, sliced through her thoughts.

"That must be Hoshi now!" Doc Woodstock exclaimed as he quickly cleaned off the thermometer with an alcohol sponge. He gave it a few hard shakes, then placed it in a container of disinfectant soap solution at the back of the treatment cart.

Lisa was close on Doc Woodstock's heels as they hurried outside.

Hoshi gave a jubilant wave as he caught sight of them. "Here she is, everyone! Practically bigger than life! The picture of health."

The mare's sleek, black coat caught glimmers of sunlight as Hoshi led her down the ramp at the back of the trailer and towards the horses' tent. Ebony held her head high. Her gait was unfaltering. Her liquid brown eyes were clear and pain free.

"Oh, Ebony!" Lisa cried, running up to her. Her heart nearly burst with happiness. "I can't believe I'm seeing you again. Welcome back!" Grinning hopelessly, laughing and crying at the same time, Lisa nuzzled her face against the mare's side and stroked her over and over.

"Looking good," Doc Woodstock declared with a nod of approval, then cleared

179

his throat loudly to disguise the catch in his voice. "Come on, ol' girl. It'll only take me a few minutes to check you over, make sure you tolerated the trip. Meanwhile, your stall's ready and waiting."

Every chance possible during the rest of that day, Lisa stole a few moments to slip back inside the horses' tent and visit Ebony, to reassure herself that this wasn't merely a fleeting dream. Seeing her again was like finding a candle that flickered brightly in a dark, empty room. Yet even the horse's successful recovery coupled with Dr. Woodstock's continued glowing assessment of her couldn't chase away the foreboding darkness deep inside.

"If I can't talk you into staying, then at least let me drive you to the airport tomorrow morning," Dr. Woodstock insisted as nightfall approached. Once again his face melted into a kind squint, yet his solemn eyes were filled with regret.

"Thanks, but I'm afraid you're going to be busier than ever now," she replied. "Taking off that much time could prove a hardship. I'll make it simple and call a cab." She forced a smile, knowing she intended to make her departure as inconspicuous as possible. She'd informed no one other than the veterinarian of the exact date and time.

Only a few days earlier, Lisa, tearful and heartbroken, had also informed him about the real reason fueling her decision. Dr. Woodstock had tried everything possible to console her, all the while muttering about the cruel realities of young love.

He patted her shoulder now in a fatherly gesture, his smile reaching his eyes. "All right, my dear. Whatever you say. But just remember what I've already told you. I don't intend to fill your position right away. If you should have second thoughts, Lisa, don't hesitate to contact our management headquarters. They'll put you in touch with me as quickly as they can."

She nodded sadly, smiling back at him. "Thanks. I *will* remember. But please don't hold out any false hopes. I'm not going to change my mind."

Morning came quickly. Overhead, the sun blazed across an azure sky. Before finishing her last-minute packing, Lisa hurried to see Ebony one final time.

"Take care, old girl," she whispered, giving the mare an affectionate pat on her velvety nose.

Ebony whinnied softly, as if indicating her own fond farewell.

"You're a real trouper, know that?" Lisa added, swiping away a tear from her cheek.

"I'll remember and love you always."

Later, as she ducked into the backseat of the waiting cab, she turned to wave at Dr. Woodstock. Thank goodness, none of the Figaros were anywhere in sight.

That morning after Estelle had left the trailer, Lisa had left her a hurriedly scribbled note, avoiding any references to Michael. "I'm sorry to have to leave so secretly this way," she'd said. "But I do hate goodbyes and I'm sure it'll be much easier for all of us."

My circus family, she thought with painful realization as the cab wheeled away. How many times before had she experienced similar heartache as she'd moved from one foster family to the next? This time, however, her parting was infinitely more bittersweet.

The cab turned into a steady stream of traffic. Unseeing, Lisa stared outside at the landmarks whizzing by. Industrial parks, housing developments, concrete buildings. They all faded into an indistinguishable blur.

Later they squealed to a stop at the passenger loading area near the United Airlines sign. Lisa paid the driver, then waited at the back of the cab while he unloaded her luggage from the trunk.

"Have a safe flight, miss," he said.

"Yes, good-bye."

As she waved him off, her mind sorted through the sketchy plans she'd made. Last night when she'd phoned Melinda back in New York, her friend had offered to share her small apartment until Lisa could find her own place again. Meanwhile, Lisa would need to update her résumé and then get busy looking for not one job, but two.

But how could she manage to salvage the pieces of her life and start over again? she wondered miserably. And most of all, how could she ever survive, knowing Michael had been banished from her life forever? At the thought, her heart twisted for the thousandth time.

"Lisa! Wait!"

Instantly she looked up. Shock waves jolted her. "Claudette! What are you doing here? How did you know?"

Michael's twin sister sprinted breathlessly up to her, weaving her way through the other travelers. "Oh, Lisa, I thought I'd never find you. Estelle told me about your note. She said you forgot your itinerary back at the trailer. That's how I knew to come to United. I was honking, trying to get your attention, but I kept losing you in traffic." Claudette stopped, sucked in a deep draft of air, and placed a hand over her heart.

"What's the matter, Claudette?" Lisa asked, blinking. A stab of fear shot through her. "Is it Ebony? Did she have a relapse?" In the entire time she'd traveled with Jessell and Stern, she'd never seen Michael's twin so distraught — not even the night she tore her leotard.

"No! It's me! It's Michael! Oh, I don't know, Lisa. It's both of us, I'm afraid." Her face twisted into a frown. "You've got to listen to me. Cancel your flight. Hold on to your luggage."

"But why?" Lisa blinked again, her mind whirling with confusion.

"Just wait till you hear me out," she pleaded. "Besides . . . you've got almost two hours till your plane takes off. If you still decide to go . . . you'll have plenty of time."

"Uh . . . all right."

Claudette ran a hand through her disheveled mane of blond hair, then touched her forehead. "Oh, my . . . I should know better than to try to run so fast."

"Let's go inside and find a place to sit down," Lisa suggested. She paused, darting Claudette a worried look. "Are you okay? Can I get you an aspirin . . . or a cup of coffee perhaps?"

"Coffee might help."

"So what's the matter?" Lisa asked again after they'd found their places at a small oval table, clutching steaming cups of gourmet coffee. She felt the tautness in her shoulders as she waited for Claudette's reply.

Michael's twin offered Lisa a wavering smile. "I know this must seem terribly cowardly of me . . . but I hope you'll forgive me once you understand the truth." Her nervous gaze angled off to one side, then settled back on Lisa again.

"Go on, Claudette," Lisa prompted softly, taking a tentative sip of coffee. She tasted the chocolaty sweetness of Swiss mocha, but the rich hot brew failed to soothe her escalating tension.

"All right. Here goes." Claudette let out a long, shaky breath. "For over a year now, I've been troubled by severe dizziness. In the beginning I tried to ignore it . . . but it didn't go away. Finally I went to our family doctor in Florida, back at winter quarters. . . ."

"And . . . ?" Lisa sat closer to the edge of her seat, inclining her head.

"Dr. Genski said it was an inner ear problem and put me on medication. Later, after the dizziness got worse, I . . . I made a long-distance call to his office to ask what I should do next. Since our next stop was

Galveston, the doctor put me in touch with an ear specialist there . . . a colleague of his from medical school." She gave an apologetic shrug, averting her gaze. "That's why Rita and I were late meeting you and Michael at the street dance. The specialist got called in for an emergency consultation, pushing my appointment back."

"So what did that doctor do?" Lisa asked. Immediate empathy eclipsed her unpleasant feelings about Claudette.

Michael's sister heaved a sigh. "He started me on a new drug, an experimental one this time. But he also said that if it didn't work, I would need to start making plans to get a replacement. I was frantic, of course. I didn't want my career to end."

"Of course not," Lisa said.

"That night at the street dance," Claudette went on, "Rita and I decided it was time to confide in Michael — and Estelle too, just as soon as we could get back to the circus grounds. But I made them promise to keep quiet till the doctors had come up with their final prognosis. That bit about adding a fourth flyer was simply a decoy, of course."

"But why, Claudette? Why would you want to keep it from the rest of your family — and everyone else too — when they might've been able to help?"

"I don't know. I . . . I guess I just wanted to hold on to what little hope I had. I figured Mom had all she could handle with Papa being gone. And of course he had his problems too." Claudette's eyes glistened with unshed tears. "But now that's all changed, Lisa. At Michael's insistence, I've told both Mom and Papa, just like I'm finally telling you. I . . . I'm sorry I waited so long. Michael's still furious with me about that."

Lisa reached out and squeezed Claudette's hand. Poor lady. No wonder she'd been acting so strangely. "Isn't there anything else the doctors can do for you?" Lisa asked.

"I'm afraid not. The experimental drug was my last-ditch effort. That night I fell from the trapeze, we knew for sure Rita would have to take my place. We also promised ourselves we'd need to practice harder than ever."

"Gosh, Claudette," Lisa gasped softly. "I thought you fell because you ripped your leotard and lost your focus."

"Hopefully everyone else did too." She took a long, slow sip of her coffee. "And when it came to our practice sessions, I hoped no one would notice that I was spending most of my time coaching Rita from the ground. Of course, that put most of the burden on Michael and my sister." Claudette stared thoughtfully down at her paper cup before adding, "And speaking of Michael, that's another reason I'm here."

"Is something wrong with Michael too?" Lisa couldn't hold back the rising panic in her voice.

"Most certainly not." A smile lifted a corner of Claudette's mouth. "Nothing more than an incurable case of lovesickness."

"Oh?" Sudden relief swept over Lisa while at the same time her stomach twisted with new dread. Was Claudette about to inform her that Michael and Rita had made a commitment?

"Last year after our stay in Madison Square Garden," Claudette continued, her voice more confident now, "Michael talked about you constantly, Lisa." Claudette went on to confess how she'd been certain Michael's real reason for leaving the circus was to go find Lisa.

Claudette took another swallow of coffee. "That was also the time I started experiencing the dizziness. I realized that if both Michael and I left, our troupe would fall apart for sure." Her eyes softened. "When my twin brother made the decision to come back, I was more relieved than you'll ever know."

"Then I came along and posed an even greater threat," Lisa finished for her. "You thought I might lead Michael astray again."

"Exactly. I know it may sound dumb, but I was scared and desperate. That's why I tried so hard to get Michael interested in Rita. I figured if he married her, he'd always stay." Claudette poked at a crumb on the table, frowning. "But I finally managed to get a grip on myself and take a positive look at life. I finally realized that though I would have to find another vocation, my life wasn't over totally."

"So what are you going to do, Claudette?" Lisa asked softly.

"I'm going to move to Montana and work with Mom's poodle breeder," she answered, brightening. "I've always loved dogs, just like you love horses. And truth is, now that I've sorted everything out, I'm really excited about my future. And luckily too, the dizziness hasn't affected my driving. Hopefully it never will."

"I'm glad your story has a happy ending," Lisa answered sincerely.

"Yes. It was a tremendous relief to realize I could still take charge of my life." Her eyes sparkled with a look of new resolve. "And

189

Michael helped me understand I also had no business trying to run anyone else's life — especially his. He told me that there'd never be any other woman for him but you. My brother's absolutely wild about you, Lisa. I've never seen him so love-struck."

The news hit Lisa like a bolt of lightning. Out of all the women Michael could have, he wanted her? No, it couldn't be true. It was simply all too confusing. She gave her head a quick shake, realizing Claudette was still talking.

"I'm sorry, Lisa. I'm truly sorry I treated you so despicably."

Lisa's thoughts reeled. "But . . . but what about Rita?" she finally managed. "You're saying Michael's not interested in her romantically?"

"No, not at all. Though in the beginning, Rita may have come on to Michael a bit at first, her interest was one-sided and short-lived. That night at the street dance when she and Danny met up again, they fell madly in love. I should say, re-fell madly in love. Rita didn't tell you they'd once been engaged."

"So they're engaged again?"

"Uh-huh. They'll be married at the end of the summer and Danny will sign on with Jessell and Stern as a drummer in our circus band. I can assure you, from now on, there'll be no one for her but Danny." She reached across the table to touch Lisa's hand. "Forgive me, Lisa? Please say you understand?"

"Oh, yes, Claudette. And I'm sorry too. Sorry I was so quick to misjudge you."

"How could you have done anything else? Especially when I treated you so badly."

"It's all in the past," Lisa assured her, meeting Claudette's contrite gaze. She put her fingertips to her temples in an effort to quiet the pounding that was growing stronger by the moment. "But what am I going to do, Claudette? I jumped to wrong conclusions about Michael too . . . accused him of some awful things." She twisted the strap of her shoulder bag and added shakily, "How can I expect Michael to forgive me too?"

"Come back with me," Claudette answered simply. "Come back and tell that to Michael."

His heart in his throat, Michael quickly elbowed his way through a sea of people. *Lisa, where are you?* he thought frantically as he gazed down the seemingly never-ending corridor. *How will I ever find you in this humongous airport?*

Lucky thing Estelle had given him Lisa's flight number and airline. At least that was one advantage. But what good was that if he couldn't manage to stop her?

Please don't leave. His thoughts raced on. *I love you. I need to tell you so. I need to take you in my arms, hold you tight, never let you go.*

He rounded a corner, dashed past two flight attendants who'd paused to talk, then picked up his pace once again. This might prove a hopeless cause. So far, he hadn't even run into Claudette. If only she hadn't waited till the last possible moment to set the record straight — though after he'd thought about it later, he'd realized he really couldn't blame her. Never before had he seen his twin sister so scared.

He dashed past an ice-cream concession and a trendy gift shop with expensive clothing in the display window, then slowed to glance down at his watch. Ten forty-seven. He muttered under his breath. Lisa's flight back to New York was scheduled for eleven sharp. Maybe she'd already boarded. Maybe it was too late.

But no, he couldn't allow himself to blow it now, he told himself as he hurried on again. He balled his hands into fists. Adrenaline surged through him. He had to find a way to keep Lisa from leaving — even if that meant forcing his way onto that plane and proposing to her right there on bended knee.

It seemed that Claudette was driving in slow motion. It seemed they'd never get back.

But when they finally did, and Claudette nosed her truck in alongside her trailer at the south end of the circus grounds, Lisa's stomach was tied in knots.

Where should she start looking for Michael first? she wondered desperately. His trailer? Inside the arena? The stabling quarters, perhaps? And when she did find him, how could she make him understand? How could she ever take back the hurtful accusations she'd hurled at him?

Quickly she wove her way down the long row of RVs and at last came to Michael's. She knocked at the door. No answer. She knocked louder and called his name, then strained her ears.

More silence.

The sun shone hot against her shoulders. Beads of perspiration dotted her forehead. A few trailers away, people mingled outside. She heard a woman's laughter. The sounds of circus children playing. Yet no signs of Michael anywhere.

Turning on her heel, she started back for the center of the circus grounds. As Lisa drew nearer, she spied Estelle emerging from the menagerie tent. She was wearing a blue-and-white floral tank top and cutoff jeans.

"Lisa!" Estelle's mouth dropped open at the sight of her. "When did you get back? Did Claudette manage to catch up with you? Did Michael too?"

"*Michael?* What are you talking about?"

"Michael took off for the airport about an hour ago to find you. He thought there was still time. He assumed you wouldn't be leaving for a couple of days yet . . . just like I did. Anyway, this morning after I came back and found your note, I rushed over to his trailer to tell him. He . . . he's trying to stop you from leaving."

"Oh, no." Lisa puffed, pausing to catch her breath. "He's got to be crazy. How does he ever expect to find me in a place like that?"

"I gave him your flight information," Estelle confessed. "He's hoping against all hope he'll track down both you and Claudette there." Estelle's eyes grew round. "My brother was nearly going crazy, worrying about Claudette's condition, longing to be with you, wanting to finally tell you the whole miserable story. But Claudette insisted she tell you first."

"I've got to go find him!" Lisa exclaimed. "Will you drive me back to the airport? Please, Estelle?"

"Don't you think it'd make more sense to wait right here? When Michael doesn't find you, he'll undoubtedly head straight back."

"Maybe so. But what if, instead, he tries to catch a flight in hopes of following me?" Lisa shook her head. "We can't wait! This could turn out to be the fiasco of the century!"

"All right. My van's unlocked. I'll meet you there in five minutes."

In no time, Estelle had disappeared from view, and Lisa, her knees still trembling in the wake of the morning's revelation, turned and hurried toward the van.

"Lisa!"

She whirled around, her gaze locking with Michael's.

Instant relief swept across his handsome face. "Lisa!" he called again. Arms flung wide, he broke into a run, closing the space between them.

"Oh, Michael!" she cried, running to meet him. "I thought I'd never see you again

. . . I thought it was good-bye forever."

"Thank goodness Claudette managed to stop you," he murmured huskily, enveloping her in his eager embrace. "I just talked to her. She told me all about it." Tenderly he twined her hair through his hands. She could feel his solid warmth and strength, hear his heart beating against her ear.

"Yes, thank goodness," she said through tears of joy. She pulled back slightly to meet his gaze. The breeze ruffled his hair, tossing a stray lock across his tanned forehead. Now more than ever, he looked so wonderfully vibrant and alive.

She swallowed hard. "I'm sorry, Michael. Dreadfully sorry. I was wrong to have said all those terrible things. About your promise to your father, about Ebony, and you . . . especially about you."

"It's all right, darling."

"But I should've realized that things aren't always as they may appear. It wasn't fair of me to jump to those conclusions."

"Doesn't matter anymore," he ground out fiercely. "All that matters is that you know and understand . . . and now you've come back." Eyes brimming with love, he pulled her to him again, crushed her against his broad chest, and kissed her long and hard.

Shimmers of pleasure coursed through her as she twined her arms around his neck and answered his kiss. She lost all track of place and time. Michael was really here. Here in her arms. Never in a million years could she have envisioned such happiness.

His voice was ragged when he finally released her. "I can't believe this is really happening. I . . . I was afraid I'd never see you again too. Darling, I'm so sorry. So sorry I couldn't tell you the truth before now. I . . . I was torn. Miserable and torn. Torn between my love for you and my concern for my twin sister."

She ran both her hands through his thick head of blond hair, reveling in his closeness. "And how could I blame you, Michael? What a predicament. And poor Claudette. If only I'd had an inkling of what she must've been going through. I can't believe how brave she's been."

"Yes, Claudette has been brave, but I admit at times she had a strange way of showing it. I promise you, Lisa, from now on, there'll be no more secrets in the Figaro family — no matter how noble the reasons. It's not worth the possible misunderstandings. It's not worth what could've happened between you and me." As he cupped her face in his hands, kept his eyes fixed on hers, his expression suddenly darkened. "You *are* staying, aren't you?"

Her answer came in scarcely a breath. "Yes, Michael. That is, if you want me to."

"If I *want* you to?" He tipped back his head and chuckled, then traced a finger down her cheek, bringing it to rest tenderly on her lips. "Oh, yes, I want you to, all right. I love you, Lisa. I want you with me always. Please say you'll join my family, become my wife. And maybe someday, if you want it too, we could start making plans to have our own little family." His eyes sparkled mischievously as he smiled down at her and added, "Don't forget, darling. Twins run in the bloodline."

Her heart was overflowing with happiness. "Oh, Michael! I love you too. I think I always have, from the very first day we met."

"So you're saying yes? You'll marry me?"

Fresh tears of joy sprang to her eyes. "Of course, Michael! Oh, yes . . . yes!"

There, right in front of Doc Woodstock, the cage boys, the riggers, the animal trainers, and others who'd quickly congregated to watch, Michael swept Lisa up in his arms, whirled her around, then kissed her again.

In the background, a ripple of applause grew louder. Then came the whistles and cheers.

"Ladies and gentlemen, children of all ages!" someone called out above the noise. "You are now witnessing the greatest show on earth!"

We hope you have enjoyed this Large Print book. Other Thorndike Press or Chivers Press Large Print books are available at your library or directly from the publishers.

For more information about current and upcoming titles, please call or write, without obligation, to:

Thorndike Press
295 Kennedy Memorial Drive
Waterville, ME 04901
Tel. (800) 223-1244
Tel. (800) 223-6121

OR

Chivers Press Limited
Windsor Bridge Road
Bath BA2 3AX
England
Tel. (0225) 335336

All our Large Print titles are designed for easy reading, and all our books are made to last.